The Man with Two Hearts

by Nicolas Osvalt

*I would like to thank Laura Delinois, "My Sese",
for all her encouragements;
and the staff of Kevin and Associates
for making my dream a reality.*

CHAPTER ONE

I DIDN'T SEE RICHARD at work today. I called him to see what was going on: no answer. It was very unusual for him. Richard always called me, even if he was running five minutes late. I left him several messages on his cell and house phone: unsuccessful. Honestly speaking, I was not in the right frame of mind. Richard had been my best friend for over twenty-five years; I had reason to be so worried. I should rephrase and say that after what Richard and I had been through, he was not just a friend; he was more than a brother to me. Friday, September 10, 2010, seemed to be the slowest day of the year, even though I was unexpectedly busy with a greater than usual number of patients. I was in charge of opening and closing the place, since Richard was not available that day. Richard and I were the proud owners of a walk-in healthcare facility called The Desired Rose, named after our spouses. Finally, I told the staff members that I had to close earlier so I could find Richard or at least hear that he was okay. I rushed to my car and drove. All I could think of was Richard. I hoped he was okay.

I drove to his apartment first. We'd given each other keys in case of an emergency, or in case one of us for some reason lost his key. We could count on one another for rescue. I looked for his car in his assigned parking spot, number 21, and it was empty. My heart raced. I didn't bother waiting for the elevator; I climbed the eight flights of stairs without taking a single breath. I rang the bell; I banged on the door—no answer. I let myself in and ran to his room. There was no sign of Richard, but there was a note on the table with my name on it.

My name is Phillip B. but everyone calls me Phil. Richard and I met at Long Island University, where we were roommates during freshman year in the fall of 1985. At first we didn't get along. He looked like someone who always wanted to be in control. I remember when he made me change sides of the room by telling me he was more comfortable by the window, even though I'd arrived at the room first and had already settled in.

Midway through the semester, two days before Thanksgiving, we had a conversation that lasted more than five minutes for the first time. I was shocked that particular morning when he approached me for advice regarding a chemistry class he was taking and failing miserably. I was happy when I told him that chemistry was one of my strongest subjects. Knowing that he was failing and seeing that he was asking me for help gave me a form of power after how he had been treating me. I also felt important and gained respect from the fact that he needed me. I helped him out by tutoring him four times a week and assisting him with his remaining homework. He managed a B in the class. He was so appreciative of my help that the next semester he introduced me to his friends and let them know that I was the reason he succeeded in chemistry. In the process we got to know each other better. Richard invited me to hang out with him and his friends, at university, at the mall, at parties, and at movies. It didn't take long for us to become best friends.

THE MAN WITH TWO HEARTS

Richard had noticed one day that I was lost for words while talking to a young lady on campus. He quickly realized that I needed a coach. Honestly, I didn't know how to approach a girl for fear of rejection. I always had in the back of my mind the feeling that I was not good enough for anyone to date me. Richard helped change that completely by coaching me to my first successful date. I was very timid, avoiding eye contact with women. Richard taught me how to overcome being shy by making me watch a videotape almost every day about the subject until I was able to follow the steps, such as smiling and keeping conversations simple. I became so confident that without hesitation I would start a conversation with anyone I liked and I would ask her out.

Richard would date girls, but it was never anything serious because he told me that he had a longtime girlfriend named Rachelle back home. One morning at about 5:00 a.m., Richard woke me up.

"Man, what is it that could not wait for later?" I asked him.

"I am in trouble," he said.

"What happened, Rich?"

"Today is February 12 and Rachelle is coming to see me. Rosie and I were supposed to have breakfast this morning. You've got to help me, man. Go take Rosie out for me. Find a story to tell her why I couldn't make it."

Rachelle wanted to surprise Richard for his birthday. She had driven from upstate New York to see him and spend the day with him. Rosie was the new flame Richard had met in the last month or two. He introduced me to Rosie one night when she came over to see where he lived on campus. Rosie was no different from the other girls he went out with; she wasn't anything serious, at least I thought so. I told him I would take her out.

Rosie lived off campus in her own apartment about five miles away. Richard was barely in the dorm since he'd met Rosie; he only came there at night to sleep. He used to tell me that he stayed late to study in the library, and I knew why he chose to stay with her once I arrived at her apartment. I wouldn't want to stay in our too hot or too cold small dorm room either. The entrance of the brand new building was breathtaking, with a large lobby decorated with exotic plants, pictures, and chairs.

As I approached her apartment, I rang the bell. Rosie quickly opened and closed the door right away, like she was shocked and afraid. I called out her name and knocked on the door again. She hesitated for a moment, and then she opened the door. The look on her face, frowning, clearly showed that she was disappointed. She was expecting Richard.

Once I was inside the door, I was already contemplating the magnificent place with all new furniture and special designer curtains. I knew right away her family had money.

"Why are you here? Is Richard okay?"

"He had to go home. His dog Lulu was not feeling well and he had to take her to the vet, so he asked me to take you out for breakfast instead."

I was not a good liar. Rosie could see that I was avoiding eye contact with her. She looked beautiful with big shiny brown eyes and a seductive voice that would intimidate anyone.

"Today is his birthday. He has to drive home to take care of his dog and couldn't tell me that himself? He had to send you?"

"Well . . . "

"Don't say another word. Come in. I am going to teach him a lesson."

I should've come up with a better lie, I thought. After all, Richard told me that she was a psychology major. She probably saw right through me. I'd never been in a situation before when I had to lie like this. I felt awkward and stupid at the same time.

"What are you going to do?" I asked.

"Well to start, this is what I have for him and now it is all yours."

She opened her robe and dropped it on the floor. I stood with my mouth wide open, like a salivating dog. I was sweating and nervous and cold at the same time. I could feel my heart beating very loud, except each beat was from my penis that was becoming erect. My eyes that had been avoiding contact were now lost in her two breasts. I wanted to devour them. Her body was that of a supermodel in the swimsuit edition. There she stood with a pink and white thong. *Is she for real?* I thought.

"Well," she said, "what are you waiting for?"

This was a big dilemma. Should I approach or should I walk away? This was my best friend's girl. My heart was beating so fast. The throbbing in my pants had almost reached its boiling point; I was ready to explode.

"Are you going to stand there all day or what?" she said in a dominating voice.

I like that, I said to myself. I followed Rosie to the bedroom. I grabbed her forcefully. I held her close in my arms. I took a long look at her for a full minute to admire her beauty. I kissed her forehead first, and then I looked straight into her eyes, where my soul, mind, and spirit—all of me—were lost. I could feel her shivering. Goosebumps covered her body as our tongues engaged in a ritual dance. I was making love to my best friend's girl. It was so good that I wouldn't dare stop. Her eyes were closed. She let me take control of her body. I gently laid her on the bed and caressed her breasts. I sucked her erect nipples in a soft and hard alternating rhythm. I stopped to watch her reaction. She was enjoying it.

"Why did you stop? Where are you going?"

"I'll be right back," I replied.

I wanted this moment to be perfect. I was thinking to be creative since the day looked like an opportunity of a lifetime. I went to her fridge and found a bottle of Hershey's syrup. I rushed back to the bed-room, poured a small amount on her left nipple, and sucked it gently. I got the tip from a movie I had watched the week before.

"Oh, don't stop!" she screamed.

I continued to pour syrup across and down her body; drop by drop, I kissed and licked until I reached her waist. I pulled at her panties and continued sucking her nipples while my fingers searched between her thighs. Her body trembled; she was screaming now, begging for more than my fingers. She was so wet.

I didn't bother removing her panties; I pushed them to one side and penetrated her gently. At first she screamed as if in pain.

"Go slow, don't hurt me," she said.

I took my time getting inside her, going slowly as she requested. I made sure I asked if it was okay.

"Yes, yes just like that," she responded.

She was enjoying it. I like to watch the facial expression of the person I am making love with. I asked her to change position so that she was on top of me. There were some discomfort at first, but in a few minutes she was riding the bull. One hand was massaging her left nipple while the other hand was massaging her clit. With each stroke of move-ment, I could see she was getting close to climax. Then she screamed loudly. I could see that she had no more energy as I finished a few seconds after her. We both lay on the bed, exhausted. We looked at each other with wonder. I felt a combination of pleasure and guilt. Rosie had a smile on her face; she shook her head in disbelief.

"What happened?" I asked her.

"I don't know if I am on Earth or in heaven," she said, laughing. "We have to do it again. I've never had such pleasure in my life. Want to do it again?"

I didn't hear a word she said except "do it again." I was thinking what a cruel act I had just committed.

"No, we won't!" I said. "What about Rich?"

"Let's not talk about him now. Come on, let's go take a shower."

For a moment I was at peace with myself knowing that Richard had a steady girlfriend. I looked at my sticky stomach and removed the condom, which had red stain on it from the syrup.

I removed it while I was looking at her then she said, "How come you brought a condom?"

"Richard told me to always have one, in case of an emergency. I had it in my wallet from the time he told me. I had no idea I was going to use it, especially today."

"Come on, let's go to the shower."

I looked at her and said, "Okay, you go first."

"No," replied Rosie, "we go together."

I became shy instantly. I was standing in front of her in the shower; I'd never done that with anyone before. I lifted my head and closed my eyes and let the water pour over me. It felt very good. The shower was large enough to accommodate two people comfortably. Suddenly, Rosie grabbed my penis.

"I've got to wash it," she said.

She bent the showerhead so water could fall on her back. She knelt down and put my penis into her mouth. I was vulnerable, trying to find something to hold on to. My back was against the wall. I wanted to scream from so much pleasure. I couldn't hold back anymore as I busted. I felt weak in the knees, but I managed to stay up. It was my turn to wash her.

I washed her back. I washed her breasts and started to kiss her as warm water poured on us. As I went past her stomach below her belly button to wash her, she gently tapped my hand and said, "I'll do that."

When she was done I turned off the water and dried her back and front and back again. She held my hand as we returned to the bedroom. She lay on her back, spread her legs, and said, "Now, it's your turn to eat me."

I had an idea of what she was talking about, but I had never done that before for anyone. Last semester I was a virgin and most of this was still new to me. The good thing was, I learned fast and followed directions very well.

I was a little hesitant at first. I dried myself slowly, pretending I didn't want to get the bed wet. In reality I was thinking of what to do. Then I said to her, "I want you to teach me what to do there. I've not done that before."

"I thought you knew what where you doing. You seemed like an expert. I have no idea either. This is my first time also," she said.

I found it hard to believe that Rich or any other guys had never done that for her before. I tried as gently as I could. She appeared to enjoy it, and I left it at that.

"Do you have classes today?" Rosie asked.

"Not until five."

"Okay," she added, "I am going to make you breakfast, and then I have to go to the mall to return some things. You can join me if you don't have plans."

I didn't. My plan was to spend time with her so I felt a duty to Richard. Rosie made pancakes with sausage, toast, and an omelet— enough to feed five people. We were so hungry. We ate them all. After such an unexpected escapade we'd just had, who wouldn't be hungry?

I felt guilty again. She didn't say anything for a while. I was wondering if she felt the same or if she regretted what had just happened between us. She knew, after all, that I was Richard's best friend.

We finished breakfast and headed out. As she was closing the door to her apartment, she asked, "How did you get here?"

"I took the campus bus," I replied. "I don't know how to get to the mall on the bus from here. Do you know?"

"No, I don't," she said. "I always drive."

We took the elevator to the parking lot in the basement of her building. She stopped in front of a shiny BMW and said, "Get in." She started the car, pressed a button, and the top rolled back. I must've been dreaming. It was my first ride in a convertible. I had so many questions, but I kept my mouth shut and enjoyed the ride.

At a red light she turned to me and our eyes met unexpectedly. It felt like Cupid had just perforated my heart with his arrow. It was like an instant fight to see who would stop the eye contact first. Fortunately for me, the light turned green. *I'm in love with Rosie,* I thought, *and I'm already in trouble with Richard. Where do we go from here?* I wanted to ask, but I didn't want to spoil the moment.

I thought I was going to the small mall by the university. She drove over the Brooklyn Bridge to FDR Drive to upstate New York's highway 87. The ride was so long I fell asleep. I woke just as she was getting off the highway to a place called Woodbury Common. It was one of the biggest malls I'd ever seen. It was brand new. She noticed that I was amazed and she held my hand while walking, assuring she was happy with the choice she made.

"You don't talk much. Why is that?" She paused. "Look, I don't want you to have any bad ideas about me because of today. After all, Rich is your best friend. I know you feel guilty about the whole situation. It was my choice. I am the slut who slept with her man's best friend because of his lame excuse and lies. Besides, I enjoyed it."

I listened attentively, and then replied that to the contrary, I felt ashamed and guilty because I took advantage of her moment of weakness. I told her that I should've resisted.

"You're full of it." She laughed. She put her right arm around my shoulder and said, "If it makes you feel better, I won't say anything to him if you don't."

We went from store to store. She was trying new clothes and asking me for my opinion. She was so sexy. I had to remind myself several times that she was Richard's girlfriend. We were in a public space and I should be careful not to kiss her where someone might see. Maybe I could go inside of one of those fitting rooms with her.

"Let's go eat lunch," she said. "My treat. Where do you want to go?"

"I like to eat anything besides campus food," I replied. "I like to eat somewhere where I can have cheesecake for dessert; it's my favorite food. I can eat it any time of the day," I added.

"How did you know my favorite dessert is cheesecake? What else do we have in common?"

We spotted a restaurant where they had a variety of cheesecakes in the windows. There was a fifteen-minute wait.

Rosie said, "I'm going to use the bathroom. I'll be right back."

I sat on a bench facing the restaurant, waiting with the waitlist pager in my hands. People passed. I was hungry. Cheesecakes in the side window of the restaurant were tempting me. A couple walked in and went straight to the cheesecake counter to order. It was Richard and Rachelle.

How could this be possible? I asked myself how Richard and Rachelle knew this place. Maybe Richard had mentioned it to Rosie, or maybe Rachelle, who lived upstate, knew about it. I debated whether I should call him before Rosie arrived or if should I pretend that I didn't see him. Just then, Rachelle turned around and noticed me.

"Isn't that your roommate?"

"Yeah! Let me go talk to him while you get the cheesecake."

"No, let me go with you," Rachelle insisted. "We can get the cheesecake later."

"What are you doing here?"

"I'm here with a date. She didn't want breakfast so we came here for lunch instead." I paused. "Remember the one I told you about? The one I told you about this morning?"

Richard didn't leave. Instead, he asked where she was.

I signaled them to come outside of the restaurant with me, pretending that I had something important to tell them.

"She went to the bathroom. She should be out shortly."

"Well," Rachelle said, turning to Richard: "Can we join them?"

I said, "Richard, can you do me a big favor?"

"What is it?"

"Remember the problem I have when I eat certain foods?"

"Acid reflux?" he said.

"Yeah! I don't want to give my date the wrong impression. Could you please get something, anything, at the pharmacy next door?"

He hesitated for a moment then said, "Sure."

"Problem solved," I said.

I went back inside. Rosie was already in the lobby.

"I saw you," she said.

"Really? I was talking with this guy."

"Stop it," she said, "I saw it was Richard. Is that Rachelle that was with him?"

"How did you know?"

"He told me he had a girlfriend back home. He said he wasn't serious with her and when you told me that he went home to take care of his sick dog I figured it out. If he went home to be with his girlfriend I gave you his birthday gift instead. Now I see with my own eyes and I am so glad I did."

"Can we go to a different restaurant?"

"Why?"

"Well, Rachelle doesn't know about any of this and I sent Richard to buy something for me to distract them because she wanted to eat with us and I couldn't let that happen."

"Maybe we should stay so she can discover what a liar Richard is," she suggested.

It didn't happen. Instead we went to a Chinese restaurant. I was having such an incredible date that I was not even hungry. Then Rosie said she had a confession to make.

"You remember when Richard introduced us the first time?"

"Yeah! I was in the dorm with my PJs on."

"As I was shaking your hand there was something I felt about you and that same feeling came back today while we were driving here. I always ask Richard about you during our conversations." She paused. "Did you know today was my first time having sex?"

I listened and stared at her quietly.

"I told Richard that I was a virgin. Since his birthday and mine fall on the same day, I had planned to give myself to him today. He didn't know that. He sent you instead. I've always liked you and I wanted to have sex, so you got his gift."

I didn't know what to say to her. I felt extra special. If Richard had known this was her plan, he would have cancelled with Rachelle. All this time I thought Richard was having sex with Rosie. All the time they were spending together, and no sex—I was shocked.

I loved her even more now. That explained the blood on the condom; I thought it was syrup. That explained why he insisted that I take her out for breakfast today: because it was her birthday too and Richard felt guilty.

CHAPTER TWO

IT WAS A school day for both of us. Anatomy was always my favorite class. I was fascinated by the development of the human body. Somehow I was not able to concentrate. I was daydreaming about how the day unfolded unexpectedly. When the class was finally over, I was scared. I had to face Richard and give him details on how the date with Rosie went. I hadn't seen him since the restaurant earlier and I didn't want to go back to the dorm right away. I went by Rosie's class, but it was already over. I went to the library for a while and sat down with my book open, only to continue daydreaming about the day with Rosie. Then I heard him.

"I was looking all over for you. We need to talk."

It was Richard. My heart was ready to explode out of my chest.

"Okay, I am finishing something here. I'll meet you at the dorm."

I was just buying myself some time. He trusted me and left.

When I got to the dorm I pretended that I was upset with him.

"Why didn't you tell me that it was her birthday? I could have gotten her some flowers instead of looking like a jerk."

"I'm sorry, man. I should have told you."

"What did you do with Rachelle today?" I wanted to know in case there was some sexual activity. At least I wouldn't feel as guilty.

"Nothing special. She got me a Movado watch for my birthday. I had to give her the gift I bought for Rosie so she wouldn't ask too many questions. She was on her period, so no sex."

"Did you see Rosie or talk to her yet?" I asked.

"No, I'll see her tomorrow. I figured I'd go to the mall and get her a gift before. What did you tell her I did today? What excuse did you give her?"

"I told her your dog was sick and you went home to take her to the vet."

"What?! Come on man, I told her that I didn't have any pets."

"What I was supposed to say, Richard? You woke me up at 5:00 a.m., and you expect me to have a good lie ready? By the way, she saw you and Rachelle at the mall. She even knows Rachelle by name."

Richard exploded. "Why did you have to tell her all my business?"

"I didn't, you did. She told me that you have a girlfriend named Rachelle back home but it wasn't serious. You showed her Rachelle's picture, remember? Why are you blaming me now?"

The truth is I felt guilty. All this time he was talking to me I was thinking that Richard would never trust me again. But honestly, who in their right frame of mind would turn down such an offer from Rosie? But I didn't want to ruin my friendship with Richard either.

As the night approached, I lay in the bed thinking of that glorious moment that we had. I thought about her smile, her body, and her laugh. Then I started to think about her panties and I got hard. I was hoping that I could see her again.

❤ ❤

The next day Richard went to see her. I was nervous and tormented. Nervous, because I didn't want Richard to find out and kill me. Tormented because I'd started to fall for her and I didn't want her to be touched by another man. I went to class, but I couldn't concentrate on anything the teacher had to say.

"What happened yesterday?" Richard asked me.

"Nothing, why?"

"I saw Rosie today and she barely talked to me. I brought her a gift. She didn't bother to open it. Are you sure you didn't tell her anything about me to make her upset?"

"I don't know what you're talking about, man. I did you a huge favor yesterday. You asked me to take her out for you and I did. Anything else you have to discuss should be with her." I continued, "Richard, put yourself in her place for a moment. You didn't show up. You sent your friend instead and then she saw you and your girlfriend at the mall. Think about it, man."

"I guess you're right," he said. "What should I do now?"

I was hoping he'd say he would dump her so I could ask him if I could date her myself. Instead he told me that she was the first woman he truly loved. He said he would do anything for her.

"Are you serious? Rosie?"

I got upset. I felt sick to my stomach. Then I burst out laughing.

"What's so funny?"

I changed my voice to sound like Louis Armstrong, "You would climb any mountain, defeat any giant, but yet you couldn't take her out yesterday morning for her birthday."

"You're not funny," replied Richard. "Here I am pouring my heart out in front of my best friend and you are making fun of me."

"What are you going to do about Rachelle?"

"I told her that I was seeing someone else."

"Really, Rich, are you crazy? What if Rosie doesn't feel the same about you?"

"Well, I am willing to have a good talk with Rosie and tell her exactly how I feel. Besides, Rosie is a virgin and I would wait until we get married to have sex with her."

I felt like punching him. I got really upset but remained calm and said, "Rich, those are deep thoughts, man. You barely know her. What if she has someone else she loves? I thought you were having sex with her all this time."

"No," said Richard, "she wanted to, but I didn't want to push it. One day we were so close to doing it, but she said it was her first time and she wanted to do it with someone that she truly loved—someone who would be her husband someday. I could wait and make that special moment for her."

"What would you do if you found out she was not a virgin anymore?" I asked.

"I love her and that would not change anything. After all this time waiting for a special someone, she would not go and have sex with anyone just like that."

I felt so guilty and ashamed. I didn't know that he felt so strongly about her. Why did she do that? Maybe she didn't know that he felt so strongly about her. I couldn't say another word after that. I pretended that I had to use the bathroom and rushed out of the room. I sat on the toilet with my hands on my face. I couldn't believe what I'd heard. I waited and hoped that he'd left the room.

"Are you okay in there?"

"I'm fine," I said. "Do you have any plans tonight?" I was trying to change the subject.

"Nope, what about you?"

"I don't know yet, but I feel like finding something to do. Maybe I'll call Judith and see what she's up to."

"Well, call her. If she's not doing anything we can go watch the game at the new place across the street."

Judith was the girl that I'd met on campus three months ago. We liked each other, but I never got too involved because we didn't really click. Girls like Judith always get the attention of men. They are ready to dump you in a heartbeat because of their beauty and ability to get anyone they want. That was why I was still thought of Rosie as a dream that came true, at least for one day, even if it evaporated like a cheap perfume the next day.

Judith was not home and I was forced to go watch the game with Richard. At least it was better than staying in the room and listening to him lament.

As soon as we walked out he said, "I seriously don't know how I am going to live without Rosie."

I guess I was wrong. He would not stop talking about her. I got so mad. I told him furiously, "Enough man, don't say another word about Rosie."

"Why are you so mad?" He added, "You're my best friend and all I'm doing is expressing how I feel. What's the problem?"

Well, you're expressing yourself to the wrong person, I thought. I was close to telling him what had happened the day before, but I didn't.

"You need to relax, man. What has changed? You rejected her to go out with another woman and today you want to marry her?"

I was trying to transfer my guilt onto him so he would leave me alone. Then I noticed he didn't say anything.

I continued, "What about Rachelle? You have been with her since your freshman year of high school and now she's not good enough for you? You dumped her for someone you met three months ago."

"Yes," he shouted, "I am doing just that. Thank you."

"Why are you thanking me?"

"I knew by confiding in you I would find the right answer," he added.

"All I was saying, Rich, is that you know what you've got with Rachelle. You don't know yet what you're going to have with Rosie."

"Life is full of surprises," he said. "You could be with someone for a long period of time and never know the person entirely. I am willing to take the chance with Rosie. I love her that much."

I had to swallow my pride. I would not say another word; otherwise he would quickly discover that something had happened between Rosie and me the day before. I came to my senses. Maybe he was trying to tell me all these things so I would confess to him. Richard was a very smart guy. I was not planning on saying anything until I saw Rosie. My hope was that Rosie would turn him down and he would go back to Rachelle. Then I would find a way to get Rosie for myself.

I went by her class. I visited all her hangout spots at school, hoping to see her. I thought of dropping by her place or leaving a note on her car, but I didn't want to bump into Richard. I was nervous. Loving Rosie was my newest torment. I became jealous. The thought of Richard with her started driving me mad. I had to wake myself from this dream. It would never become a reality. I was desperate for love; I was desperate for Rosie.

When I got to the dorm I saw Richard. He looked a bit down. I knew it was cruel of me, but instantly I became happy. Maybe Rosie dumped him.

"What happened man? Why are you looking so down? Are you okay?"

"I spent some time with Rosie today and all she was asking about was you."

"What do you mean she was asking about me?"

"I told her how I felt. I poured my heart out to her. She asked if I'd told you how I really felt about her. I think she developed a sort of thing for you after you spent the day with her."

"Don't be crazy, man. Maybe she thought I was a loyal and true friend to you. Are you jealous, Rich?"

I tried to downplay the situation by teasing him. It was obvious that Rosie hadn't told him we had sex. Maybe she was testing to see if I'd told him something. I couldn't take it anymore.

"Maybe she wants to have sex with you," I said.

Richard got upset. He got up and said, "I told you she is a virgin and I will not have sex with her until we get married."

"Well, Rich, people have needs. Don't you have needs? You can go and have sex, but you are saving her for marriage. Maybe she is trying to tell you something and you are ignoring her."

Richard turned to me and softly said, "Be honest with me. Did she say anything to you the other day about wanting to have sex?"

I thought for a second and said no.

Richard then continued to say that he was a changed man. He was in love with her.

"I am willing from now on to devote my life to her. I've talked to a lot of women on campus or elsewhere, but I am a big pretender. I charmed them by talking to them, but I've always used moral judgment when it comes to certain thing, a lot of things. That was one of the reasons I let go of Rachelle. I love Rosie more and it would not be right to keep them both."

I felt so ashamed. I didn't know how to answer him. Now I really regretted having sex with Rosie. He made a lot of sense. I was upset with myself. If he were in my place he would not have done it. I lay down on the bed and covered my head, trying to forget about what happened between Rosie and me. I finally fell asleep.

It was 5:30 a.m. when Richard shook me awake.

"Wake up, wake up."

"What is it?"

"I couldn't sleep," Richard said, "and our friendship is too big to ever let anyone, especially a woman, come between us. I came up with a set of ideas that we could use as a guide to our friendship."

"What are you talking about?" I said.

He pulled out his notebook, shifting pages. He stopped, went back, and continued forward, then stopped halfway into the notebook.

"I've got it," he yelled. "I came up with ten rules that we should use, if you agree with me. You can add or remove as you wish, too. After each rule you should tell me if you agree or disagree. Okay?"

"Let me hear them," I said.

He went on, "Rule number one: We should never date or sleep with one another's girlfriends, even after one of us stops seeing that person. For example, even though Rachelle and I broke up, you should never date her."

I wanted to tell him to go to hell, but I knew where he was going so I said I agreed. I thought he suspected that Rosie might have a thing for me, so he wanted to be at peace with the situation.

"Rule number two: Our girlfriends should be also be friends. It should be our job to make sure it happens, even in the case of personality conflicts."

I agreed.

"Rule number three: If we have a problem with our girlfriends, we should solve it—the four of us."

"I don't get that," I replied.

"If you have a problem with Rosie, me, you, your girlfriend, and Rosie should sit down together and solve it."

I said, "I don't know about that one, but I guess yes."

"Rule number four: We should keep no secrets from one another."

I agreed. I thought to myself, *What is this? What is he talking about? He let the horses out and now he is closing the gate. Too late, fool.*

He read number five. I didn't hear him and I didn't bother to ask him to repeat it. Honestly, I didn't care what he was saying and I said I agreed.

"I think five is enough," I said.

He said, "You don't even want to hear the other rules?"

"It doesn't really matter. I'm not interested. I don't understand what you're trying to accomplish. What would happen if I violated them or if you violated them?"

He said, "I know that you would probably not understand why I am doing this. To me it means loyalty. I want to know if I can trust you or count on you as my best friend."

"Wait a minute," I said. "Why are you being so paranoid? What have I done to you? You woke me up and asked me to take your girlfriend out while you took your other girlfriend out and now for some strange reason you have rules."

I continued, "Remember last year? Your number one rule was never to fall in love. Are you really in love, man? If you really are, more power to you, just leave me out of it. Go tell it to them. One more thing: Next time you want to play, you're confused, or don't know what to do, or you're in trouble, leave me out of it. Don't ask me to take your girlfriend out."

I lifted my head up in a pissed-off kind of way, covered my head, and went back to sleep.

❤ ❤

I was not able to sleep. I had to see Rosie to find out what she'd said to Richard to make him so paranoid. If she hadn't said anything to him, then he was definitely suspicious. I began questioning myself. Maybe someone saw us and reported it to Richard. Maybe at the mall she was hanging on me like I was her boyfriend. Who could it be? I had to find Rosie and talk to her about this dilemma. Maybe I should stay away because if for any reason Richard caught me with her, I would be screwed.

I had a biology test the next day. Since I couldn't sleep I went to the library to study for that test. For some strange reason I felt even the trees on the campus were sad. I didn't even eat breakfast; I was not in the mood. I went straight to my favorite spot. I sat down for a good ten minutes before I finally opened my bag and pulled out the notebook that had my biology notes. A piece of paper fell out on the desk. The note said: "Meet me by Morgan's Hall at 5:00 p.m. today." The note instantly changed my mood.

I felt like I had drunk ten bottles of an energy drink. I was ready to conquer the world. I wanted five o'clock to come right away. I started to think that it might be a trick from Richard to find out if Rosie and I were talking. I didn't care. I needed to see her anyway to talk to her.

I went back to the dorm and took a shower. I wore the same thing I had worn the day I went to Rosie's house. I was nervous. This was unbearable. I got to Morgan's Hall at 4:30 p.m. I sat in the lobby checking my surroundings to make sure it wasn't a trap. Morgan's Hall was a newer building, erected two years before I came to the school. It was supposed to be the tallest on campus and the most technologically advanced. The lobby had many pictures of inventors along with some large modern art statues. Every time the big swinging doors opened I was expecting to see Rosie. I had already prepared a speech in case Richard walked in. I needed to use the bathroom, but I didn't dare move in case she arrived. Five o'clock finally arrived. I was looking at the entrance when she came in.

"We can't stay here. Let's go to my car," she said.

I followed her to the parking lot. She had on a colorful top with a black miniskirt. Two beautiful long and sexy legs in a pair of high-heeled shoes completed the look. I thought, *Did she come to school today or was she out working as a model?*

We got into her car. She drove out of the parking lot and asked me if there was somewhere I wanted to go.

"Anywhere we can talk."

She said, "I know a great place. I passed it last month when I was going to my aunt's house. By the way," she added, "I don't wear any underwear."

I felt a throbbing in my pants again, stronger than the first time I was in her apartment. Good thing I was sitting down and not walking around; otherwise people would've seen a massive erection. It was so unexpected to hear that from her.

I said, "I'm wearing briefs."

"Let me see." She reached over with her right hand, massaging my hard cock over my pants. "What have you been feeding that beast?"

My eyes were closed. I was enjoying the ride. Suddenly she pulled into a spot over a hill. You could see the lights of another town in the distance. She let down the top of the convertible and turned the car lights off. She came around to my side of the car, opened my door, pushed my seat all the way back, opened my pants, pulled my dick out, and started to suck it.

I started to moan in pleasure. Then she opened her legs and sat on top of me. I grabbed her breasts, put one in my mouth, and gently sucked with each stroke. I placed my hands on her hips and sucked the alternate nipple. The position became uncomfortable, so we stepped out of the car. She leaned on the trunk and I came up from behind her. I took off my pants like I was in her bedroom. I lifted her miniskirt and inserted my hard, beating cock into her vagina. I was in heaven. I was so close to coming and I didn't want that to happen. I wanted her to come first. I stopped, turned her around, sat her on the trunk, and spread her legs. I'd learned a new word that day in my human sexuality class that was in my head all day, and I finally had the opportunity to employ it: "cunnilingus."

She was enjoying it. She held my head with one hand while the other hand held onto the car. I felt her come in my mouth. It had a warm, slippery, and salty taste. I brought her down from the trunk and returned to the same position as before.

She said, "Make sure you pull out so you don't get me pregnant."

When I finished, I put my pants on and she opened the trunk and got a towel to wipe herself. She grabbed some underwear and put them on and closed the trunk. She sat down in the driver's seat, turned around, and looked at me.

"That was the last time you and I will have sex."

I was surprised to hear that. I thought she was joking. I laughed and said, "Why?"

She was serious. "Did you hear me? I meant it."

"Okay, as you wish dear," I replied.

She reached in the backseat and took out a pair of sneakers. She put them on and placed her high heels in the back. I said nothing for a moment. She started to drive. I felt used.

I said, "What is this? We came to talk and instead we fucked. Then you tell me this was the last time we're having sex. What is this? Stop the car if we're not going to talk. I will find my way back."

She realized that I was serious. She made a U-turn and went back to the same spot where we'd just had sex. She stepped out of the car and walked over to the edge of the hill. I followed her.

"What's the matter?" I said.

"Richard and I came here the other day. We were standing right here when he pulled out a box, got on one knee, and proposed to me. I gladly said yes to him. You see, I love Richard. He is the type of guy that I see in my future as a great husband. I feel so bad. He knew that I was a virgin. Look at me here falling so much in love with you. I look at you and I know you will break my heart. If you really care about me, about us, please let me have a chance to make it work with Richard. Stay away from me, even if I try to contact you. Please ignore me. Could you, would you do that for me, please?"

I was hurt. I had so much that I wanted to say to her. I was in love with her, too. I thought so much about her. I loved her. I felt that I was going crazy, but swallowed my pride and said I would do everything possible in my power to respect her wishes. I would not interfere.

"Good luck to both of you." I went back to the car.

She followed me and said, "It's not like that. We're still going to be friends, right?"

I said, "What's the use? It will only cause heartache and unfinished memories. You said it yourself: I have nothing to offer you."

"We're supposed to get married six months after graduation. I want you to be there, I want you to support us. I would never mention us to anyone. I am counting on you to do the same."

She dropped me off near campus. I went to the library and was thinking how stupid I felt. I knew it would never have happened between us, but that didn't stop me from dreaming about her every day. She was spontaneous. I liked that. I was already missing her and not even an hour had gone by. Richard and Rosie belonged together. I had to find ways to get her out of my head and move on. Everything was clear. Richard was acting weird because he had proposed to her. It made no sense to me, but then that's who Richard was.

CHAPTER THREE

THE LAST TIME I saw Rosie was May 16, the last day of my fresh-man year. I was thinking about her the whole summer. Staying away from her was torture to me, but I managed to keep my promise to her. Sophomore year, I barely saw her on campus unless she was hanging onto Richard. They made me sick sometimes, kissing in front of me. I was glad, though, to see that Richard was happy. He told me himself from time to time that being with Rosie was the best choice he had made in his life.

I didn't go out with anyone since I was so focused on school and didn't want my heart to be broken again, like Rosie had broken it. My school advisor told me: "You have to declare a major at Long Island University. As a junior you can't stay undeclared." I was taking classes related to science. One of my goals was to become a doctor. I spoke with my guidance counselor and told her of my goal. She explained all the options available to me, including how many years of school and internships I had to complete. I wanted to have a profession where I could work right away and help my mother with my younger sister, I told her. Unlike most of the students at the university, I had to rely on financial aid, scholarships, and loans to pay for my tuition.

My father passed away when I was seven. I still remember when he used to take me to the park every afternoon when he came home from work. We used to run and fly kites when it was windy. Every weekend, he would take the whole family to the mall for movies and ice cream. I constantly thought about him. My mother moved with my sister and me to a small twobedroom apartment in Newark, New Jersey when I was eight. I quickly understood the importance and value of hard work, especially for a single woman like my mother. I saw how difficult it was for her, struggling with the bills. I always told her that I would take care of her someday. She would work from early morning to late at night. Sometimes we never had a chance to see each other for days. I felt bad when I knew how hard my mother was working; she had two jobs to provide for my sister and me. Medical school took too long, I told her. The counselor suggested nursing, physical therapy, or occupational therapy. I chose nursing.

The guidance counselor explained that I would graduate with a bachelor's degree, then take the state board exams, and then I could start working within two to three months after graduation. She said my student loans would be cheaper to repay. I listened to her advice and I went to the nursing department to register for nursing classes.

❤ ❤

During junior year, Richard and I, along with two other guys, lived together in a different section of the campus. The space was much bigger, so we didn't have to share rooms anymore. Rosie had left me several notes at the beginning of the semester under my door, asking me to contact her, but I ignored them all. She rarely came to that new place when I was there. I always managed to make sure that I was never alone with her when I used to see her, so we didn't have to talk. The feelings I had for her were different. I was hurt because I loved her. The way she had treated me during our last rendezvous made me upset. What she did was unforgivable. Rosie looked better and better each time I saw her with Richard around campus. People knew they were an item because you rarely saw one without the other. Sometimes we used to go out in a group of friends; she would come along with Richard. Rosie would make conversation and openly ask why she didn't see me anymore. I always answered simply.

❤ ❤

In junior year, in fall 1987, I registered for sixteen credits, only for nursing classes. The classes were part lecture and part clinical. On Mondays and Wednesdays, I was in school all day. Tuesday and Thursday and part of Friday morning I was rotating from a hospital to a nursing home for clinical. The teacher arranged a small group of students to have a preceptor. A preceptor is a nurse who we had to follow, to learn from, and basically work with during the hospital rotation.

The first week, the teacher introduced me to my preceptor, Desiree. She was the nurse on the east wing of the hospital. Desiree was to be my preceptor for the next nine weeks. She walked in the room and introduced herself. I said to myself: "Is she a nurse or a supermodel?" She had a short white dress that revealed two long legs, along with two large breasts that made it difficult to maintain eye contact without a quick glance. She had a beautiful, flawless face with a voice of an angel.

Desiree went to a community college and received her associate degree in nursing. She was twenty-two, a year older than me. I was very nervous around her. I think she noticed my sweating hands. She told me that I was in good hands and she would be sure to teach me everything that she knew.

Having a preceptor meant I had to follow Desiree everywhere, except to the bathroom. We took breaks together, even ate in the cafeteria together. By the third week, we took lunch breaks out of the hospital because the weather was nice and that gave us an opportunity to explore other delicatessens in the neighborhood.

We became so accustomed to each other that she was telling me about her life story. She even told me that she was in love with her first boyfriend who broke her heart so bad that she was being careful not to let that happen again. I told her about my life story too, but mostly regarding my admiration for hardworking women, just like my mother. She was so touched by my story that she reached across the table and held my hands. She found me very humbled. I never mentioned Rosie, of course.

By the seventh week, I was so comfortable that I made a daring move that could have gotten me expelled from the school. During lunch I told Desiree that I was attracted to her and I wanted to take her out to a movie. She didn't answer the question. Instead she said: "We have to go." She didn't say anything to me for the rest of the afternoon. I couldn't believe the mistake I'd made.

All I could think of was how I would defend that action to my teacher. I could point out that it wasn't a crime to be attracted to someone. Fortunately, the teacher never said anything to me. This made me happy and less anxious about the situation. There were only two weeks left with Desiree and she would not see me again after that.

The following week, our eighth week, I was very nervous about seeing Desiree. I didn't know what to expect. I prepared an apology about my behavior to Desiree. The teacher at the start of the clinical day always had a meeting with us students before we went to our preceptors. The teacher dismissed all the students except me. She asked me to wait for her. I was anxious—my heart was beating out of my chest. *I'm in trouble*, I said to myself. But all she wanted was to tell me that I was going to pair up with another nurse named Yvette because Desiree was off. I was disappointed I wouldn't see Desiree.

I couldn't wait for November 18 to come, the final day of our first hospital rotation. I thought about Desiree; I felt really bad for asking her out. Besides, I wasn't thinking straight. Why would an established woman want to go out with me? I had nothing to offer. I was still a student. I used that as motivation to take on a different perspective about my work ethic.

I was the first in my class to arrive early on that last morning. I went to the hospital's cafeteria to have breakfast. I had a good half an hour before I had to report to the day shift nurses. The truth was that Desiree always started her morning routine there; I was hoping to see her. I felt a tap on my shoulder. It was Desiree.

"I am running late. I have to float to the northeast wing today."

She gave me a folded piece of paper and left. As I was about to read it, the professor walked into the cafeteria. I put the note back in my pocket, stood up, and went to the room for our final morning meeting. Afterward, I went to the restroom. My heart was beating fast; I was so anxious to read Desiree's note.

The note read, *I couldn't talk to you last week but I will gladly go out with you this weekend*. She included her phone number. I was the happiest man on Earth. As soon as I got to the dorm at the end of the day, I dropped my schoolbag on the floor and went straight for the phone. I called Desiree. We spoke briefly and at the end of the conversation we agreed to meet in the mall on Saturday, November 21, 1987 at 6:00 p.m. My official first date with Desiree.

Richard was in his room with his door wide open. He lay on his bed. I didn't even notice him until he asked what was going on. I explained the whole thing to him. He was very delighted. I had a date, which meant Rosie was off my mind for now.

The last time I'd gone out with someone was with Rosie. I was nervous and shy during the date with Desiree. I found myself unable to coordinate words and lost all confidence that I'd once had when I met a girl. Desiree realized I was so nervous and she held my hand.

She said, "We are outside of work right now and outside of school, so don't be nervous. We are here to have a good time. Just relax and let's have a good time."

I bravely took her hand, lifted it up to my mouth, and kissed it while I looked straight into her eyes. I was nervous because she was older and more mature than the other girls in school. I regained my confidence and took control of myself after I saw her blush. I had never seen such a dazzling smile in my life, I told her.

The date proceeded smoothly. We ate and then we went bowling, and later we watched a movie. During the movie, all I could think of was how I was going to get back to the campus. I didn't have a car and the last bus to the campus departed at 12:00 a.m. I hadn't asked Desiree how she got to the mall and I wouldn't dare ask her for a ride. I resolved to stay at the bus stop until the first bus arrived at 7:00 a.m.

When the movie was over, I asked her where she was parked. I walked her to her car. It was the only car on that side of the mall. She unlocked the car as we walked toward it. I didn't say anything; I was waiting for her to offer if she could drop me on the other side of the mall. Then I would tell her that I didn't have a car and ask if she would drop me by the school. She instead went toward the passenger side, opened the door, and handed me the car keys. She sat in the passenger's seat. I thought to myself, *What is it with these women and BMWs?*

"It's a nice car," I said.

Her car was the latest model, a 525. I drove myself to campus. When I stopped she was asleep; I hated to wake her up. Earlier she had told me where she lived, so I drove her to her apartment complex.

"We're here." I gently took her hand and said, "Desiree, you're home."

She got up suddenly and said, "Aren't you coming?"

She directed me inside her apartment. I followed her. I noticed that she was very tired and barely able to keep her eyes open. She changed clothes, keeping her underwear on and putting on a small shirt. She looked comfortable. It was like we'd known each other for years. I felt a cramp starting from the top of my head all the way down to my penis. It was like being struck by 10,000 volts but only one spot in my body got all the impact: my penis.

I had to tell my penis to calm down, to come down. At the same moment, it went back down, as she lay in the bed. I pulled the cover over her, turned the light off in her room, gently shut her bedroom door, and went to the living room. I made myself comfortable; I felt that because we were talking for nine weeks during clinical she had become comfortable with me too. I took off my shirt and my shoes. I went to the kitchen, got a can of soda, got a sheet out of her closet, turned the TV on, and went to sleep on the sofa.

I slept until 9:30 in the morning. Although the couch was not the best to sleep on, I was happy just because I was at her house. I sat for a few minutes, still dreaming of a great time I had with her yesterday. From the first moment I saw her, I had the feeling that something great would happen between us, but not so quickly as this. I was thinking of me being at her house. We had not even kissed yet. I put my shirt back and went to take a peek at her door, and found she was still sleeping.

I went to the kitchen, and I saw that she had everything I needed to make breakfast. I made pancakes with strawberries and whipped cream, and a spinach omelet with cheese because she mentioned while we were eating lunch one day that it was her favorite. I made smoothies with fruits and vanilla ice cream. Then I set the table and knocked at the bedroom door and walked in. She moved over on the other side of the bed, and I lay next to her.

"Good morning. I made breakfast," I said.

"You did? What did you make?"

"Let's go eat," I said.

She went to the other side of her bedroom, and got a robe out of her closet. I was still sitting on the edge of the bed, admiring that curvaceous and well-designed body crossing in front of me. I felt like pulling her over, sitting her on my lap, and making sweet love to her. But I got up and followed her to the kitchen.

"Who taught you how to cook?"

"Breakfast? I usually use my imagination. Anything else, my mother," I said.

We sat for an hour. We ate everything. She enjoyed it and I was so happy. We talked, joked.

"I've never done that before—bring anyone in my house, especially after the first date, but with you I feel there is a special connection."

"I've been feeling the same way too," I said. "Could it be fate?"

I wanted to tell her that she was the second person who made me feel that special kind of way, but instead I said: "You are very beautiful. The first time I laid eyes on you, I felt a shivering sensation from my head, through my spine, and all over my body. I knew right away that we were connected."

She said, "Does it matter that I am older than you?"

I said, "Who's counting?"

"So, you like older women?"

"No," I replied, "I like the right woman."

"What is a right woman for you?"

"The one I can spend all day with, go to sleep, and wake up feeling the same way about every day for the rest of my life."

"Men often get bored. You will too."

"I can't say I know what will happen tomorrow, but I know I am very loyal. I love with my heart, not with anything else, and as long as the heart is sincere, there will be room for only one thing: love."

"Would you cheat on me?"

"No," I said, "my heart beats one beat at a time and each beat is for only you."

At the same moment, I was thinking about Rosie, my secret love. I knew that I was not the cheating type, but I knew the way I felt about Rosie. She was the only woman that I would forever love. The only woman that I would like to have but I couldn't have. I realized that it was a good choice being with Desiree because I noticed with Rosie that the love was not reciprocal. I knew I had to seal my heart to someone else and let Rosie be who she wanted to be, and be with who she wanted to be with. Desiree became the perfect fit for me at a perfect time.

Desiree noticed a moment of silence and said, "What are you thinking about?"

"Nothing, just thinking how lucky a man I am to meet someone like you."

She added, "I can tolerate a lot things from a man, but I can't deal with cheating. I love with all my heart and expect to get the same in return, nothing less. I would rather stay by myself instead of sharing my heart with another woman."

"With me, you never have to worry about that," I said. "I am exactly your mirror image when it comes to the heart."

I wanted to go off that love and heart business because it was not appropriate at that moment. At any given moment, any slip of the tongue, any careless word could mean the end of us before we even started. I wisely changed the subject when I remember she'd mentioned yesterday that her back was hurting her.

"How's your back?" I said.

"Okay." Then she added, "Do you want to give me a massage?"

"Yes." My tactic worked. "Sure, do you have any oil?"

"Yes, in the bathroom, in the medicine cabinet."

I didn't see any oil except something made out of pomegranate. I took a small portion, poured it in a small glass container, mixed it with baby oil, and warmed it up in the microwave enough so she could feel the warmth of the oil.

I walked to the bedroom. She lay on her belly. I was looking at a flawless masterpiece lying in a thong. I didn't know where to begin; it was obvious that massage was no longer on my mind, but banging that sexy body.

I dimmed the light in the bedroom. She was listening to a soft love song but at that particular moment, I was thinking about Marvin Gaye and sexual healing. I rubbed my hands with the oil and applied it on her soft body where visible goose bumps were seen. I was getting hot and sweating, so I removed the t-shirt that I had on. Really what I wanted to remove was my underwear that had become uncomfortable with a massive erection I was having. I quickly was done with her back. Honestly I had no idea what I was doing because my mind was lost in her beautiful body.

I said, "You have to turn around so I can do the front."

She turned and I said to myself, *to hell with massage.* I kissed her on her forehead. I kissed her tenderly on her right cheek. The next one landed right on her lips. She was ready for more. I unhooked her bra from the front and gently massaged her breasts with the warm oil while leaving the nipples with no oil so I could use my tongue to add that sensual vibration. We made good and sweet love until late afternoon. We moved from the bedroom to the kitchen to the sofa and ended in the shower, where we were both clearly exhausted. That was the second best day of my life that reminded me of the first time Rosie and I had made love.

We went back to the bedroom and slept until about 9:00 p.m. I remembered that I had to study for the pathophysiology test the next day. I explained the situation to her and she said, "Well you can study here. I can help you."

"I don't have any books here and my notes are in the dorm," I told her.

"Take the car go get all your stuff. I am going to make space in the closet for your clothes."

"Did you ask me to move in with you?"

"Yes," she said

The offer sounded too good to be true and I didn't know how to politely turn it down. Besides, I didn't want to be anybody's puppy, to have someone tell me when to come, what to do—well, except Rosie's. I told her that I had to go home for Thanksgiving. Then I said:

"Don't you think it's a little too early for us?"

"I am the type of person who always follows my good instinct. I have been praying, 'God, guide me to the right guy.' He gave me all the signs I needed, so why wait?" Then she added. "Go home and think about it. When you come back, if you change your mind I will understand.

"It's just a suggestion. I figure that you will be more comfortable here with me. I am sure you will have more space here, and you can save your parents the extra money that you have to pay for room and board."

She jumped on top of me, started to kiss me, and said, "Besides, you have me here all to yourself twenty-four hours a day."

It didn't take much effort for me to accept Desiree's offer. All thoughts came to my mind while driving, including the boys on campus, my mother, how they would take this news. When I got to the campus, I called the guys for an emergency meeting. Good thing it was a Sunday night with few activities besides studying, so they all rushed to hear what the emergency was. I told them that I had a new girlfriend who lived alone. I probably would spend most of my time with her but would be still on campus too sometimes. I showed them her car, and they were very happy for me. One of them told me, "If you don't want to go I could take your place."

Richard helped me bring some of my stuff to the car. He told me to leave some in the dorm in case something happened and I had to return. We gave each other a hug and he told me he was proud of me. I drove back to my new home, where a set of keys was already waiting for me when I arrived. I called my mother; I told her that I had to study. I would stay on campus and I would not be able to come for Thanksgiving; she understood.

Monday, I drove her to work and went to classes. I went to my room in the dorm and saw Richard and Joe, one of the other roommates.

"How was your first emancipated night?" they asked me.

I told them it was very nice for me; I felt bad for them that they had to sleep alone. We were just kidding around. Richard stood up and tapped my shoulder.

"My boy just became a man last week," he said sarcastically.

I went home at the end of the semester. I stayed for a week and returned to my new flame Desiree right after the New Year.

Desiree and I got along very well. I was so very happy that I'd met her. She was the part that my life was missing. We made love every early morning, when we were off during the days, and every night before we slept. Whoever got up last would make the bed and whoever got up first prepared breakfast. Afternoons, we cooked, ate, and cleaned the dishes together. We became a real couple. I started to forget about Rosie, or at least thought about her less than I was thinking about her before.

February 12, 1988 was Richard and Rosie's birthday. They had planned to have a big party. They rented a space for the occasion not too far from the school. I was invited the first day after the winter break. While we were out one night, she told me in front of the guys to make sure that I came to their party. She wanted to make sure I showed up. She also put an invitation under my door at the dorm. It said, "You better be there, I'll reserve the best dance for you. I miss you so much and I can't wait to see you." I read the card and destroyed it right away.

I told Desiree about Richard and told her that he and his girlfriend were celebrating their twenty-first birthdays and we were invited. She was exited to finally meet with my friends. By then rumors had already spread to Rosie that I had a girlfriend. Honestly, I was nervous. I still loved Rosie because if Richard were to dump her right at that moment, in a heartbeat I would've run and rescued her with my heart, even though she broke mine.

Everyone was waiting for me at that party. The boys wanted to see the woman who stole my heart enough to make me spend all my time with her. Rosie wanted to see who I was coming with. I guess she wanted to compare.

The guys were so happy for me. We shook hands and I was showing off my girlfriend to everyone. I saw Rosie across the other side of the room, with her brother and Richard. I walked to them with Desiree while holding her hand. Richard hugged me.

I said to Rosie, "This is my girlfriend, Desiree."

Rosie smiled at her, shook her hand and said, "Nice meeting you. You are beautiful."

She turned and said to me, "Richard is working on the sound. I have a cake and a few other things in my car. Can you give me a hand getting them, please?"

"Of course," I said.

I took Desiree to a seat and told her that I would be back shortly.

As soon as we were away from the place Rosie said, "How could you? You have some nerve bringing this woman to my birthday party! Out of all days, you choose today to humiliate me. Well, thank you, you have succeeded."

I said, "Weren't you the one who told me to stay away? Weren't you the one who told me that Richard proposed and you said yes? Don't I deserve to have someone to love me who I can propose to?"

"Don't you dare do it tonight," she said.

"Why not? Tonight seems to be the perfect night. We made love and then you told me to leave you alone. I should do it tonight and make you feel what I felt that day."

I looked at the backseat of her car and said, "Where's the cake?"

"At my house," she said.

"Oh no!" I said. "There's no way I am going to ride in that car alone with you. Besides, I have my girlfriend sitting and waiting for me. I don't want to put anything on her mind. Give me the things that you have. Go get the cake yourself."

"Is this how you're treating me now?"

"It is what it is," I answered.

I took the few cups and plates that she had in her car and went back inside. I sat next to Desiree, who was already interacting with the other guys. Richard came over and asked me to help him with one of the decorations.

I said, "Rich, today is her birthday too. Rosie shouldn't be the one getting the cake at her house."

He said, "Her friend was supposed to bring it, but had car trouble so Rosie had the cake delivered to her next-door neighbor. By the way," Richard added, "I proposed to Rosie, and she said yes. We are going to announce it tonight."

I knew already, but pretended to be shocked by the news and congratulated him. He said it would be an honor for me to be his groomsman. I politely declined the offer.

He said, "It's going to be after graduation. You have some time to think about it. By the way, I have to give it to you: Desiree is beautiful and if she's as nice as she looks, you should keep her."

"You have no idea," I said, "I am already in love with her." I continued, "Rosie is the perfect choice for you, too."

"You think so?" said Richard.

"I know so," I said.

"My family and friends are saying that I am too young to be in the marriage business.

You don't think so?"

"What do you mean, Rich?" I asked.

"They suggested waiting after graduation, finding a job, then proposing to her."

"Waiting for what, man? I've observed you and Rosie a couple of times at the school and at the house. I can truly say that she is ready, comfortable, and the ultimate choice for you. Both of your parents are rich, so they would definitely get you guys a head start if needed."

"Do you know she is still a virgin and we are not having sex until that planned honeymoon?"

"No! You are kidding," I said with the most rotten conscience. "Are you sure that hot girl is still a virgin, man?"

"She told me before and we're not having sex, but as you know," Richard added, "this is not the reason I want to marry her. Frankly, I couldn't care less if she is or not. I love her."

After hearing that from him, I felt a stabbing pain straight in my heart. I was thinking about the ultimate betrayal. Looking at him, I saw he was so innocent. At least I was happy that Rosie knew I had someone and everything was really over between us: no more poor Richard. After I met Desiree, I didn't have to live with the guilty feeling anymore. Believe it or not, I had to end it with Rosie although in my heart she was that rare stone that was irreplaceable.

As the party was jamming, I was dancing with my new honey. I heard someone say, "He promised me a dance." It was Rosie asking Desiree if she could dance with me. She was dancing with Richard close by where I was.

"Sure," Desiree said.

Rosie handed Desiree to Richard for a dance and she held my hand and disappeared onto the dance floor. She had timed the whole event carefully, because as soon as we started to dance it was a slow dance, "Lady in Red." She held me so close. I couldn't control my erection. While dancing, she slowly put her hand on the crotch of my pants. She was massaging my cock. I was starting to enjoy it when I remembered Richard and the talk we'd just had. I thought of Desiree looking for me and finding me in a compromised position. I pulled away.

"Did you feel it? Was it hard enough for you?"

She said, "Yes, I want it in my mouth right now."

I said, "Too bad that was the last time I will ever get so close to you. I hope you enjoyed it." And I walked away.

CHAPTER FOUR

AFTER ROSIE'S BIRTHDAY PARTY, I didn't hear from her again. She must have learned from Richard that I was living with Desiree. Richard told her everything; they had no secrets whatsoever. He even told her everything about the girls he used to meet before her, including Rachelle.

I wish I could say the same about Rosie because she had kept me a secret from Richard all this time. Richard always told me whenever I came across him at school that Rosie still asked how I was doing. She suggested several times to Richard that we should double date. I always politely declined. I would say that I was busy with school or I would say that Desiree had to work. Rosie was trouble and I should stay away from her.

It was senior year. Everyone was looking forward to May 24, 1989, graduation day. For the past year and a half, Desiree and I had gotten along so well that I had almost forgotten about Rosie. My mother knew that I was kind of seeing someone but I didn't tell her that we were living together. I didn't even go to the dorm anymore. Desiree and I were so great together. We always made time for each other. We had breakfast and dinner together. On days that we could, we would have lunch out, sometimes at the mall. Desiree had not been looking good lately. She was constantly complaining of a weird smell that she suddenly noticed on me. I would shower twice some nights before she would let me sleep with her. She didn't want me to make breakfast anymore. She was vomiting for two days. She felt so bad that she didn't go to work most of the week. I began to worry. I encouraged her to make an appointment to see her doctor.

On the day we went to the doctor, I could see her face was pale; she barely could talk. The doctor ordered blood tests and gave her a prescription for nausea. He told her that he would call her when he got the results back. Later that afternoon, I made chicken noodle soup and I was feeding her with crackers. The doctor called. I quickly handed the phone to Desiree. I purposely had the phone on the speaker.

"Did you take the pills I prescribed for your nausea?"

"No," said Desiree, "I didn't yet, but I will soon."

"Don't bother," the doctor said. "I want you to come and get some prenatal prescriptions. You are pregnant. Congratulations."

I wished I didn't have the phone on speaker. I didn't know what to say or how to react. I knew that I was not ready to be a father. As soon as I realized she was about to hang up, I went to the bathroom. I was scared.

As I came out the bathroom, Desiree said, "We're going to have a baby."

I went to her. I kissed her and sat down next to her quietly.

"Are you scared?" she asked.

"I am not," I said. "I have to drop out of school and work. I can always go back and finish later."

"Don't be silly," Desiree responded. "I have enough money saved. I shouldn't worry. Besides, you're about to graduate and you will be able to work."

She sat down next to me and said, "I love you."

I turned around, kissed her on the lips, and said, "I love you more."

I couldn't sleep. I was thinking about how I was going to tell my mother. I hadn't even told her yet that I had a serious girlfriend. I had to find out how to break the news at once to her: school, moving in together with Desiree, and the pregnancy. Never mind my mother, I had no idea how to take care of a baby. I saw them during my maternity rotation: tiny little things, so fragile I didn't want to even hold one, for fear of mishandling it. The thought that I was going to be a father became a scary one. I went to the living room to watch the television while Desiree was still sleeping. Nothing interesting was on, or my mind was not into watching TV at that particular moment. I needed someone to talk to, someone I could trust. I called Richard. It was 3:30 a.m.

"Are you awake?" I asked him.

"I am now. What's going on?"

"Can I trust you with something?"

"Of course," Richard replied, "with anything. You are my best friend."

"Desiree is pregnant and I don't know what to do."

Richard stayed quiet for a moment. He was shocked.

"Congratulations. It's great news. You should be proud. Besides, Desiree will be a great mother."

I listened to him for a while talking about everything else.

"You've got to marry her. I can get you the money for the ring. You should propose to her. Then go to city hall and we can have a small ceremony party for you guys afterward."

We spoke until 6:00 a.m. I told him that was a great idea but I would get the ring myself and I thanked him for the offer. I was still ashamed of what I had done to Richard. He was such a great friend to me.

I went back to the bedroom and before I lay on the bed I took a good five minutes to admire Desiree. I never really took my time to see what a beautiful woman I had. Knowing she was going to be my wife and carry my baby, I felt a rush of pride and relief. I knew I'd made the right choice to be with her. I lay on the bed and pulled her close in my arms to kiss her. I rubbed her stomach.

"What are you doing?" she said, half asleep.

"I am welcoming our baby. I just want him to feel the hand of his father and let him know that I am here for us."

"How do you know the baby will be a boy?" Desiree asked.

"I already know." I added, "Besides, from now on, I want you to say 'our baby.'"

I held her left hand. I carefully stepped out of the bed and knelt down on my right knee. I pulled out a ring of my pocket.

"Desiree, from the first time we met, you became a part of me that I can't live without. You are a rare stone that is irreplaceable to my heart. There's nothing more I want in this world than to spend every moment with you. Will you marry me?"

Desiree was shocked because it was so unexpected. To be honest I was shocked too that I asked, but it was worth it after all she had done for me and I truly loved her.

"I will marry you. I love you so much. I love you. What a surprise!" she added.

The ring was my mother's. She never wore it. Last time I went home, I saw it and I told her I was going to sell it and get some money for it to buy books. She did give me permission. I never mentioned to anyone that I had a ring to sell, and never had the chance to go to the pawnshop. Now I was so glad I'd kept it.

The ring fit her finger perfectly. My mother was not the jewelry-wearing type. She rarely used to wear it, maybe once a year. I called my mother the next day. I said to her that the ring fit perfectly. She asked me whom I'd sold it to and how much I'd gotten for it. I told her I gave it to Desiree. I told her the ring was priceless because I proposed to her with the ring. I also told her that she was pregnant. For some reason, she thought that I was kidding and asked me to bring it the next time I came home.

When I turned sixteen, my mother sat me down and gave me a lecture about girls. Since I'd been in college, her lectures were regarding "the right woman." She always emphasized the importance of education before marriage. My mother and I had a great relationship. I would never want to disappoint her. My mother thought that I was still a virgin. She told me last time that it always good to wait until after marriage, but if I had the urge to make sure I used a condom. That was the reason she didn't believe the story about Desiree when I told her she was pregnant.

I told Desiree that we would be visiting my mother for Easter. By this point, my sister had spoken several times with Desiree, and they were very excited to meet each other. I knew my mother would be happy that I had someone, and disappointed that I was going to be a father before finishing school. I realized how hard she was working, late nights, six to seven days a week. I wanted to help her out, especially with my sister who about to start college next year.

I was very unhappy with myself. Not because the baby was coming, but because it was a bad time. I was not ready emotionally and financially. I hated the fact that Desiree was the breadwinner of the family. As a man it did not feel right. I was not able to focus. I thought about my situation with Desiree and with my mother, and with myself not even graduated yet. I always wanted to have a family, but I wanted to graduate first, then become financially secure, and then start a family.

I loved Desiree; the fact that I woke up every morning and saw how happy she was having me by her side was the ultimate reward.

When Desiree and I found out about the pregnancy she was already in her third month. At almost five months now, she clearly had started to show. She wore a dress that made it obvious. She loved being pregnant. My mother would've had a heart attack if she had met her the first time with that dress. I politely explained to her that since it would be the first time meeting with my mother, and she didn't know about the pregnancy yet, it would be nice if she would agree to wear something else.

The plan was to get to my house very early on the day before Easter so we could take my mother and my sister out for breakfast. Desiree felt so sick and hungry that we had to pull over and we ate at a diner along the road. When we arrived my mother had already gone to work. I called her and told her to meet us for dinner at one of her favorite restaurants. She didn't want to, but I insisted by telling her Desiree was with me.

The restaurant was a better strategy in case my mother had something negative to say; it would be less offensive in public. I loved my mother and Desiree both. I valued my mother's opinions, but now as a grown man I had to accept the challenges of life. It was also one of the most important things for me to have my mother get along with whomever I chose to love. I knew my mother could be overprotective when it came to my choices. I hoped when she met Desiree she would be happy for me.

"Wow! Son, I see that you have gained weight."

This was the first thing my mother said when she saw us. She looked at Desiree and said, "What are you feeding my son?"

She laughed.

"I've heard so many good things about you from my son," she said.

The truth was that I had not said much to my mother about

Desiree. I knew then she was trying to make Desiree feel comfortable.

"You're very pretty," my mother said as they kissed one another on the cheek.

While we were eating, my mother noticed the ring on Desiree's finger. She quickly realized that I was not kidding when I told her about the ring and Desiree being pregnant. All of a sudden it looked like my mother had lost her appetite. She gave me a look, and I quickly understood that she knew Desiree was pregnant. Before she said anything I told her that Desiree was more than a girlfriend. She was my future wife and she was going to be a grandmother.

"Congratulations to both of you." She was shocked.

My mother believed in the choices that I made with my life. She was not worried that I wouldn't be a great father. I was happy knowing she said the right things and Desiree was smiling to hear that I would be a great father. I reached over to my mother's side and gave her a kiss.

Later, at her house, I couldn't sleep. I went to the family room to watch TV while Desiree was sleeping. Ever since she became pregnant, we rarely had sex. Every time I got close to her she always said that she was not in the mood. I was lying on the sofa watching TV when Rosie came to mind. I thought about the brief moments we spent together, the way she was around me; I got hard. After having sex almost two to three times a day, then once a week, and now none, it was easy to get aroused. I quickly got up, turned the TV off, and went to see if I could get lucky tonight. Desiree was sleeping so deeply. She was lying on her side, so I lay next to her, put my hands around her belly, chased away those crazy thoughts I had, and fell asleep.

I woke up early the next morning and went to my mother's room. I wanted to get her opinion regarding the whole situation with Desiree. Somehow I thought she had more to say to me. I kissed her and sat on the bed next to her. She asked me if I was okay. I said I was. She proceeded to say that she knew this was a big step, an unexpected step, but she believed that I could handle it.

I heard the disappointment in her voice. She never believed this would happen to me so fast. She was worried about my future and whether I would finish school. I told her that the dream I had would not be shattered by these circumstances. I would continue to make her proud. She didn't answer. I quietly left.

There was always an atmosphere of joy when I came home, but not this time. My sister Ann came over and said, "I am going to be an aunt. I can't wait, Desiree told me." She then added, "She is beautiful." My mother went to the room to talk to Desiree while my sister and I made breakfast. I had class and Desiree had to work early the next day, so we left in the early afternoon on Easter. She was very happy that she went to meet my family, she said. I asked her what she and my mother had said earlier. She wouldn't tell me. She said, "The only thing I will tell you is that I really like your mother."

Each day, as the belly was growing, so was my love for Desiree. She was so kind and so good to me I could never ask for a better partner. Although we were not having sex as before, the coming of the baby brought us closer together. Every afternoon when we had time, we were walking from mall to mall. We had visited all the baby stores in the area. We reserved most of the weekends for painting, name choosing, and gathering baby supplies. My mother rarely called me, but she was calling Desiree two to three times a week to check on her. I was very happy about the way they got along well.

The phone rang. It was Desiree's father. Mr. Benjamin Patterson was a well-known lawyer in the town. Desiree told me that ever since she was young he wanted her to be a lawyer. She was never interested in law, and he barely talked to her during the end of high school. Being the only child, he also didn't like her choice of boyfriends during high school. He always gave her ultimatums to stop seeing boys he didn't like or she would be on her own. Desiree was hurt by what he said. She did things on her own. She took out loans. She went to the community college and finished an associate degree in nursing. After her parents divorced, her mother got remarried and moved to California. They talked at least four to six times a week. I spoke to her mother several times; she was a very nice lady. She knew about Desiree's pregnancy. Maybe she was the one who had informed her father about it.

I answered and immediately could tell he was arrogant.

"Whom am I speaking with?" he said.

"Who is calling?" I said, wanting him to introduce himself first.

"Tell my daughter, Desiree, I called."

And he simply hung up, saying nothing else. I spoiled Desiree's afternoon when I told her that her father called. She called her mother to find out if she knew why he had called. Her mother said that he was her father and that he had a right to call her whenever he pleased.

Desiree said, "I don't know what he wants from me; we haven't spoken for almost a year and now he wants to talk to me? I'm not calling him."

I said: "Your mother is right, he made a step by calling you today. You should call him back."

"I will do no such thing," she replied.

I went and sat next to her. Then I said, "I would do anything to see my father once more, but he is dead. I know if he were alive we would have gotten into disagreements, but that's what parents are for."

She gave me a tender kiss on my cheek, took the phone, and called her father.

"How are you honey, I've been expecting your call."

"I'm fine," responded Desiree. "Last time we spoke on the phone you told me that you don't have a daughter. I managed my life as if I had no father. Now that I am pregnant, you are the last person that I expected to see or hear from."

"Honey, I am sorry for everything. I will be in town next week; it will be a great pleasure for me to see you again, and talk and put our differences aside."

Desiree agreed to meet with him the following Saturday and told him that she would bring me to meet him.

Desiree was exited. She loved her dad. She warned me that he was the type that thought no one was ever good enough for his daughter. Mr. Patterson was already at the restaurant waiting for us. He was so happy to see Desiree that some people in the restaurant turned to watch their interaction, which lasted almost two minutes before they finally sat down.

Desiree said, "Dad, this is Phil, my fiancé."

He extended his hand for a quick shake and didn't say anything.

I said, "Pleasure to meet you, sir." He didn't respond.

Desiree told him that I was attending Long Island University, and would graduate May 24. He didn't answer her.

He was more focused on finding out about Desiree's wellbeing and was trying to make up for lost time with her.

Honestly, I felt out place. Every time Desiree included me in a conversation, he shook his head briefly and changed the subject.

Suddenly, Desiree excused herself to go use the bathroom.

I took the opportunity to have a conversation with him. He banged his hand on the table, looked at me, and said: "I love my daughter very much. She could've been anything she wanted if it weren't for punks like you who have come into her life. If you lay one finger on my daughter or hurt her in any way, I will personally kill you."

I was about to answer him, but Desiree walked out of the bathroom. I said to myself that I would have another opportunity some other time to answer him. He asked the waiter for the check and I told the waiter to make it separate. I would pay for Desiree and myself.

As we were leaving, he pulled Desiree to the side and told her that he had a trust fund and some money put aside for her. Desiree said that she would think about it. He said, "With that money you can get yourself a nice house for the baby." She didn't answer him.

I went to get the car from the parking lot while he was talking with Desiree. I left without saying anything to him.

"I saw that you were very mad when I came out the bathroom. Did my father say anything to you?"

"No," I replied, "was he supposed to say something?"

"Sometimes he can be mean."

She asked if she should take his money. I didn't want to show her that I was interested in her because of her father's money. I told her it was up to her and said I wanted nothing to do with her father's money. After I told her that, an argument started, but we quickly made up and agreed not to talk about it for a while.

Desiree and I agreed to apply for a marriage license two weeks after meeting with her father. I called one of my cousins to be a witness and Desiree brought her best friend from junior high. We managed to keep it secret because we both judged it was necessary to keep our parents out of it.

Desiree and I went to city hall and got married on Friday, April 21, 1989. I went and told the guys that Desiree and I got married. They got together that afternoon, invited her to dinner, and had a little party for us. I could say honestly that Desiree had changed a lot of things in me. I saw myself as more mature now. I found myself looking forward to coming home to be with the love of my life. Richard felt that he should've been there, but I had my reason, and its name was Rosie.

Richard and I went to the deli across from the school that had our favorite sandwiches and we were talking. It was our last talk regarding everything face to face before graduation. I still felt remorse for sleeping with Rosie. I was at least happy when Richard was talking about how much he loved her. I was able to talk about Desiree and how good she was to me. We talked about old times and how fast four years had passed. We talked about future plans, but we swore to one another not to let anything come between us, to keep our friendship and be there for one another.

Richard had broken my heart. He apologized for the way he was behaving after I went out with Rosie that day. I did not say anything; I knew I was wrong for keeping such a secret. He trusted me. I should've followed my instinct and not had sex with Rosie. He was loyal to me. I was glad to put everything behind me with Rosie. Richard told me that he and Rosie were truly in love and couldn't wait to be together like I was with Desiree.

As soon as Richard told me that he and Rosie were in love, something rose up inside. I was forced to assess my situation with Rosie. I felt that I had put a punishment upon myself for no reason. I couldn't talk to anyone about it. Some nights I couldn't sleep. What had I done to Richard? He was the only person who would have listened, but I could never speak with him. He was the real victim.

As we were about to sit down and eat, Richard asked: "Did you ever like Rosie?"

"Yeah!" I said. "But just like a sister." I added, "She is your girlfriend, and we are like brothers. I wouldn't see her any other way."

I was never a good liar but when it came to Rosie I became pretty good at it.

Richard said: "She likes you, and," he added, "not like a brother. That was the reason I've gotten so paranoid. I was so jealous to see that she liked you more than me."

"That's not true," I said, "Besides, remember for her birthday when you asked me to take her out that day? All she was talking about was you. She was very upset after she saw you with Rachelle. She cried about how much she loved you, but I promised her that I would not tell you she cried that day."

I continued, "Maybe she wanted to get back at you for Rachelle. Maybe she wanted you to be jealous and know how it feels? Richard, women are like that. Maybe she wanted you to be jealous so you could devote all your attention to her. When you knew she liked someone, you would do whatever she wants you to do. Guess what, it worked. Wasn't it that same night that you came up with your friendship rules?"

Richard said, "You're right, I went so crazy that week. I dumped Rachelle. I was so paranoid. She kind of put crazy thoughts in my head that day, like she really liked you and she had the best day of her life with you."

I said to myself: "Rosie is good. She manipulated Richard to dump Rachelle so she would become the one and only. That woman is strange and that's one of the reasons I am fascinated by her." I wanted to stop talking about Rosie so he didn't have any idea that things between Rosie and me were more than what he knew.

"Have you heard from Rachelle?"

"Oh yeah! She called me from time to time to see if we could reconnect, but I was never interested again. She wanted us to meet one more time so we could see if there were no more feelings between us. I told her that would not solve the problem because I knew already that my heart belongs to Rosie."

"I was always curious to ask you: what made you change your mind so quick about Rachelle?"

"Maybe it was the distance, and we weren't seeing each other as much as when we were in high school. From the time I met Rosie, everything I had for Rachelle was gone. I wanted to settle down right away with Rosie, while I never managed to tell Rachelle that I loved her once in the relationship.

"I hope she never breaks my heart. That would kill me if she ever did one day," added Richard.

We hugged and shook hands. He wished me good luck with Desiree and my marriage and told me to make sure we saw each other for graduation so I could meet his family.

CHAPTER FIVE

MAY 24 FINALLY ARRIVED. I graduated with a bachelor of science degree in nursing. I was very proud of my accomplishment. I was very happy also to hear the contentment in my mother's laugh. She invited several of her friends and family members to the ceremony.

Desiree's belly was big—in fact, she was seven and a half months pregnant. It looked like she was ready to give birth right then. I took the occasion to tell my mother that we went to city hall and got married. She was furious about it, but in the end she was happy that I had someone. Desiree was my wife and most of my mother's friends who knew and my family were shocked when they saw Desiree's belly. One even said, "At least he was able to study too." Desiree and I just laughed, because my mother could see that we were in love.

Graduation day was also a sad day for me. I had to say a final goodbye to Rosie. We were looking for each other for those special few minutes together. She was with her family when I saw her. She called my name and excused herself to her family and ran to me.

THE MAN WITH TWO HEARTS

Rosie followed me to a spot where we were able to speak openly. Although we were next to small gatherings of friends and families of other graduates, we hugged each other. We didn't say much. Tears poured out of Rosie's face. I gave her my handkerchief. As Rosie wiped tears from her face, she walked away, and said, "I love you."

She walked away so quickly back to her parents that I didn't have a chance to tell her that I loved her too. I had a feeling Richard had told her everything between Desiree and me.

Richard was looking for me so he could introduce me to his family. Someone screamed my name and when I turned around it was Richard with his arms open wide to give me a hug.

"We did it! We did it!" Richard said.

He introduced me to his family. Wonderful people. Richard was the mirror image of his father. He invited me to a big barbecue he was having that weekend. I told him I would make it if the Mrs. had no plans. He laughed and said, "I can't compete with that." I took Richard to meet my mother and my sister Ann. He hugged my mother and thanked her for giving him such a special friend like me.

That night I couldn't sleep. I was reminiscing about everything. Most of all I was thinking about Richard and Rosie. Richard's kindness tormented me, especially what he said to my mother. We would laugh and it was great in the moment, but then I'd feel like a hypocrite. Richard didn't hold back any secrets from me and I hid mine from him. Richard had been thoughtful. He was thankful that I had been his roommate, patient with him, and grateful that I had taught him chemistry.

As days went by after graduation, I found myself in love with Rosie and unable to ignore the fact that we'd had sex—not just once, but several times. The hardest part of it all: I couldn't talk to anyone about it. Who in the world would understand these matters of the heart? A situation so delicate, so dangerous, it could rip a solid friendship apart.

I wanted to call Richard and tell him so I could free myself of this burden. In order for that to happen I had to make sure that I would never have to speak to or see Rosie again. I was madly in love with her even as I prepared to make Desiree my wife. I found myself daydreaming of Rosie's panties and making love to her again.

Desiree and I weren't having sex because of her pregnancy, which made my mind wander. I needed to focus on the fact that I was going to be a father. I needed to put Rosie out of my mind before somebody got hurt. I got up from the couch and I went into the bedroom. I lay next to Desiree, wrapped my arms around her belly, and fell asleep with her in my arms.

The next day I started to make plans for my future. I had to study for my state license exam and I had to make arrangements for my baby on the way. I'd been living off of Desiree and I felt that it was time that I started to provide my share. She never gave any impression that she was unhappy with me for not providing, but I was unhappy about it. My mother didn't raise me not to be the breadwinner.

I made several calls asking about employment opportunities and I found something in a liquor store. I planned to work, study, and prepare myself for my state license exam.

I was never too crazy about the town. It was okay for school, but it was not an ideal place for a family. Desiree agreed. I told her that after passing the state license exam, I would find a nursing job. Then I'd save money to buy a house in an ideal neighborhood for a family. Desiree immediately took up the hobby of house hunting.

Desiree found a house in the Hudson Valley area, in New Paltz. Her father, then, wrote her a check for the cost of the house. It was the best newlywed present anyone could give. We never had to worry about a mortgage.

On July 22 at 6:00 p.m., Desiree gave birth to a healthy, nine-pound boy after twelve hours in labor. We named him after my father, Bryan. I was so happy. I was in the hospital with Desiree and was able to see all the agonies and suffering that she went through. That, along with being raised by my mother, had made me more appreciative of life and women. After I cut the umbilical cord, I held this small treasure in my arms and promised to be there for him always. Richard and Rosie visited us the same afternoon. They stayed with us for a whole week; they helped fix up the nursery. Rosie was a great help to Desiree. Finally I was happy to see that we'd buried the past. She was happily married to Richard.

I passed my license exam two weeks after Bryan was born. I got my first job as a visiting nurse a month later.

Over time, I kept in touch with Richard. He visited and stayed with us some weekends alone; sometimes he brought Rosie. He had gone back to New Jersey and moved in with his parents. Richard graduated with a physical therapy degree. He had taken his board exams and planned to obtain his doctorate degree.

Rosie planned to continue to get her doctorate in psychology. Richard was very happy having Rosie as his wife. Rosie had considered several schools, including those near my house. I prayed that never happened. She had considered a school near her parents' house in Boston instead.

The following spring, they planned to have a big wedding. Richard told me that Rosie then threatened to leave him if he didn't have sex with her. They went to city hall and got married. Rosie travelled between Richard's apartment and her parents' house. They didn't know Rosie was already married. Rosie let them plan her a big wedding for the following spring.

I had a feeling that Rosie could see the love between Desiree and me. So she decided to let go. One weekend, exactly three months after

Bryan's birth, they visited. I needed to do the grocery shopping. It was early Sunday morning. Richard was still sleeping, and Rosie asked me if she could come along.

"Sure," I said.

I was so glad because I had an opportunity to talk to her. That was the first time that I didn't see us taking any sexual actions. Although the previous times were unpredicted, I felt that she and I had become more mature about things.

As soon as we left the house I asked her, "How is marriage with Richard?"

"Great, he is a wonderful husband," she said.

"I feel the same about Desiree," I said.

We talked for a while, and she told me about her plans. We reminisced about college. Then she said, as I was getting out of the car, "I've missed you. I truly do."

I looked at her. I wanted to tell her how many wet dreams I'd been having about her, but instead I said, "If we were meant to be, it would have been you with this baby. But as you see, not everything we wish in this life always comes true."

I continued, "Having Bryan, Desiree, you, and Richard as friends makes me the richest man on Earth. Let's build a new and improved future, where we will not hurt our loved one ever again, as a pact. Do you agree?" I said.

"Yes! You are right," she said

We shook hands on it and went inside the supermarket.

CHAPTER SIX

ALMOST EVERY MONTH, Rosie and Richard visited us. Bryan was nine months old. They loved him and spoiled him by bringing expensive toys for him every time they visited. Sometimes during weekends, we would take Bryan to my mother's house or my sister would come over to my house. Desiree and Rosie (who were now best friends), Richard, and I would go out to places like Atlantic City, dancing, or just to have a good time. One thing that I was very happy about: Rosie had respected the agreement and didn't try anything on me. I didn't think much about her anymore either. I was very happy to see that things between Rosie and me didn't turn into a devastating fiasco. Instead, it solidified our friendship. One Sunday afternoon, as we were having lunch, Richard and Rosie broke the news to us that the wedding would be June 4. We were the first ones invited and he would not take no for an answer: I was the best man. Richard and Rosie said that they had another surprise for us. "What is it?" Desiree and I asked together.

"Well, Rosie and I have seen how hard you guys have been working. Between the house, work, and Bryan, you two never take some vacation time. You got married at city hall and didn't even have honeymoon. We want you to come to Hawaii with us during our honeymoon. You would have a separate room and we would just spend a week with our friends. We'll consider it your honeymoon too."

I hesitated for a moment and said: "Rich, this is your time with Rosie. We can go on a vacation together next year." Then I added, "We can't leave Bryan for a whole week like that."

"Don't you worry, my friend, that's why I called it a surprise," he said. "I already spoke with your mom. She said she would be glad to take care of Bryan for you. Besides, Rosie and I have already purchased the package for four."

Desiree hugged Rosie, thanked her, and Richard said we would go with them.

I felt guilty; Richard was too good for me as a friend. I was thinking that maybe Rosie put him up to this. I didn't want to go, but if I insisted, they would suspect there was a motive behind my thoughts.

❤ ❤

Rosie and Richard's families had combined to make the most fantastic fairytale wedding for their children. It was an outdoor affair next to a lake. There were a lot of exotic plants, and even peacocks were at the site. Richard came on a white horse and dressed as a prince and Rosie was definitely the princess of the night with the longest white wedding dress, sitting in a carriage transported by four men. She looked as exotic as the plants. I was lost looking at her. I said to myself: "She is finally gone, I can close my heart forever." The wedding had more than 250 people attending. They took time taking pictures with everyone. I was exhausted by the end the night and couldn't wait to start that well deserved vacation with my wife, and my friends Rosie and Richard. The two families gave them a Rolls Royce as wedding gift. I guess the logo represented their first initials.

The thought of seeing Rosie all night very happy and exotic looking had recreated lost moments again. I was glad to be going away together with them for a whole week. How excited I was. I also had to be careful not to show any form of interest so Richard or Desiree didn't have any suspicion, so I was complaining about how long the flight was going to be.

That first time Rosie and I had made love would be eternally engraved in my mind. We made love at least four to five times that first day. I would have given anything to turn it into reality again. It was torture to be in love with two women at the same time. Some people say that could never be true because there will always be a preference, but not to me.

On the flight to Hawaii I had the opportunity to sit between Desiree and Rosie. I had one leg forward so my foot could touch Rosie's foot. I knew it was senseless and I probably should have kept my distance, but I wanted to feel her.

We arrived on the island early in the morning. We immediately checked in. The package deal had us in the same hotel with different rooms and there were minor changes in the tour. The first day we were so tired that we slept almost all day and afternoon and missed the island tour. At breakfast the next day, Richard said he wanted to tour the island anyway so he rearranged his schedule to go. Unfortunately, they only had space for two, not four, because we missed our turn the day before. Desiree and I told Richard to go to the tour with Rosie and we would go swimming instead.

Rosie said, "I am not going, I want to go swimming."

Desiree tried to convince her to go and said, "Rosie, this is your honeymoon, there will be no other tour. Just go with him."

"He should cancel it so we could do something else," she said.

I said: "I would go with you, Rich, but you know this was never my thing."

Desiree said, "Since the tour means so much to you, okay Richard, I will go with you."

Problem solved. Rosie didn't mind having Desiree take her place on the tour and I agreed to go swimming with Rosie. I didn't see any harm in it.

Richard was very happy. Rosie was clearly disappointed that Richard hadn't stayed with her. She sat on the bench as the people gathered and left for the tour.

My heart was beating fast. Since Rosie and I were alone, especially in Hawaii, anything could happen, even though time had changed us. We had a pact and had been respecting it. I would do anything not to let anything happen between us. Rosie and I walked along the beach and talked. She put her hand in mine.

"I've missed you so much," she said.

I had the same thought. Did she orchestrate this so we could be alone? I pretended that I didn't hear her. Instead, I asked her about her parents and the new home she and Richard had moved into. She ignored my questions.

She stopped and jumped in front of me. I couldn't take another step.

"Didn't you hear me? I said I missed you. I truly do," she huffed.

"I miss you too, but you and I know it's not right. You're on your honeymoon with Richard, who is my best friend, and the godfather of my child. Don't you think we've hurt him enough?"

She stood there for what must have only been a few minutes, but it felt like time stood still. Her face took on a look of relief. Maybe she finally understood that what we had been feeling was wrong. I finally stood up for Richard. I felt for that moment the torment I was suffering would finally be over. I was talking sense, but my body was telling me that I was a fool.

Rosie was silent. She pointed at a sign announcing we'd arrived at the beach. It was early and it looked like we were the first to arrive. I ran into the water and went under an incoming wave. The water was slightly cold; it was refreshing. When I came up for air she was standing in front of me.

Rosie had on a long white t-shirt; she wasn't wearing a bra. Her nipples were visibly erect. She wasn't wearing any underwear either. She opened her arms and embraced me. Before I could say anything she had her tongue dancing in my mouth. I lost all lucidity. At some point my swim trunks had come off; I can't remember when. I pulled her legs toward me, holding her thighs, and inserted my penis inside her.

It was her fantasy to have sex in the ocean and here we were making it come true. We weren't too far from the shore, so I was able to stand on both feet. We made love, sweet love. It was such a perfect moment for us; we passionately screamed.

Rosie and I had a special connection that went beyond sex. Although I made love to my wife all the time and we had sexual relations before we were married, it still wasn't the same as with Rosie. The pureness and the dominant passion that surrounded Rosie and me made it so difficult to see our relationship as just sexual.

Rosie was the best lover I'd ever had. Each moment I spent with her, although it always seemed to be the last, represented the best. I was already in search of the next great adventure with her. I was looking to hold her in my arms again and again.

This moment on the beach was the best sex I'd had with her. I didn't use a condom. I didn't know this was going to happen; there was no way to plan for it.

I lost my shorts in the process. It's a good thing there was no one around. Rosie gave me her towel to wear during the walk back to the hotel. I couldn't believe what had just happened. We barely said anything to each other on the walk back.

The sun made me dizzy; my body was still buzzing and I started to have an erection again. To distract from it I picked up a leafy pink china rose on the side of the trail. I placed it in her wet hair. She smiled and thanked me.

When we reached the hotel she checked if Richard had returned. He hadn't. She followed me to my room and as soon as the door closed and the safety lock was on I dropped my towel. I had already reached my maximum level of erection. She wanted to do it on the bed, but the bed should be exclusively for my wife and me, I thought. After all, I had some sense of morality.

We started on the chaise and when that became uncomfortable, we lay on the carpeted floor. My heart was racing. I feared we'd be caught. She closed her eyes while on top of me, her head tilted back; I was holding her hips, alternating the rhythm with her breasts.

She was enjoying it; she didn't seem to care about being caught. Unexpected sexual encounters are often the greatest, or so it seemed. We tried many different positions; my favorite was when she lay flat on her back; while my penis was inside of her, I was massaging her clit at the same time. Or when we reversed the roles and she lay on top of me with her back to me; my right hand was massaging her clit while my left hand was playing with her left breast. We were aware that each time we made love it could be our last time. We knew it was wrong, but who was judging?

After what seemed like hours, we were exhausted. We slept on the floor naked and wrapped around each other. It felt right, like we belonged together. We weren't asleep for long, maybe about a half hour. Rosie awoke and quickly got up.

"I've got to go," she said.

"We need to sit down and talk. We need to come up with a better way to meet. We can't keep sneaking around."

She agreed.

We decided to have lunch and talk. She went to her room to clean up and get dressed. When I arrived to pick her up for lunch, she opened the door and was butt naked. I knew better; we would have started going at it all over again, so I waited outside. She wore a long, light blue and sheer dress. Every curve of her sexy body was visible. We walked hand and hand as if we were on our honeymoon. Once in line for the buffet she leaned back onto me and whispered:

"I know you've been looking at my body. I have no underwear on."

I looked back to make sure Desiree wasn't around. I reached down and touched her ass; it was true. I gently pulled her back and pressed my hard erection against her.

"You're bad, so bad that maybe we should skip lunch so I can punish you."

The offer was tempting, but I declined. I said I was hungry, but in fact I knew we didn't have enough time. I wasn't sure when Desiree was coming back and I did not intend to get caught.

We found a table away from all the activities at the resort where we could talk without raising our voices. I moved my chair so I could sit next to her instead of facing her at the table, so I could feed her. She enjoyed it.

"Where do we go from here?"

"I truly don't know," she said. "There is something special about you; I've never felt like that with anyone in my entire life, including Richard. I am very aware that we're doing the wrong thing, but I always find myself thinking about you—lately more than ever. I feel jealous when I see you with Desiree. I know I shouldn't feel that way, but I can't help it. I think I am making the biggest mistake of my life by being with the wrong man. Where do we go from here? I don't know."

I looked around to make sure no one was coming and I gave her a big kiss right on her mouth.

"What do you think happened that we have to hide our love?"

"I've never seen you as the husband type. You gave me the impression that you were a heartless player."

I stared at her, dumbfounded and confused.

"I won't let any man break my heart, but I knew I was in trouble the first time I saw you." She smiled. "I think Richard knew right away that I liked you too."

I took her hand.

"I told him once that when I am around someone who I truly like tears run from my eyes. When we met I was crying. I told you it was an allergy, but I don't suffer from allergies. That was my first clue."

I listened intently. I didn't know what to say.

She continued, "You made me so nervous. I couldn't look you in the eye. I remember my heart was beating so fast it felt like it was skipping beats. I had a tingling sensation between my thighs. I am always a self-confident woman who takes crap from no one, but I always feel so vulnerable around you. I didn't know that was going to be the case until today, otherwise I would've, I should've listened to my basic instincts and been with you."

She paused.

"It wasn't like this with Richard. I told him that I never felt too strongly about him, but he convinced me that he could prove me wrong. He is the greatest guy I know, but you have my heart. I've always felt something missing with him, but I love him," she added. "How do you feel about Desiree? Be honest."

"I love her. She and Bryan are the greatest thing in my life." As I said it, her face took on a somber expression. I felt that I had broken her heart, or her expectation.

"Ever since the morning I went to your house, I've never spent a day without thinking of you. I was willing to sacrifice my friendship with Richard. I almost told him the truth about us. Each time I came close to doing it, I remembered the promise I made to you. I have kept that promise."

I continued to tell her that there were nights I spent awake thinking about her. I made it clear that it was too late for us because we each had someone who truly loved us. We had to stop having these moments. I was afraid that we'd eventually get caught and it would be devastating.

She got up. She had not finished eating. She didn't say a word. She just turned and ran back to her room. I tried to catch her. I followed briskly so as not to draw attention to the situation. I didn't want anyone to notice something was wrong. I caught up with her in the lobby waiting for the elevator.

She was crying. I said I was sorry. Before the elevator door opened, she held my face with her two hands and gave me a long kiss.

"I promise I will stay away from you for good."

And with that she got on the elevator. I felt that I had lost a precious gift. I wasn't sure I'd made the right decision by telling her that we should stop seeing each. I didn't even have a chance to tell her how much I loved her. We could've been so great together. My head was about to explode. I loved her and also my wife. I wished I had the power to combine them into one. They both made me happy. They both were beautiful, kind, and sexy. I began to realize that I was a man with two hearts.

I never imagined that one day I would be in love with two women at once. Life is full of contradictions. Sometimes it is difficult to find one person to truly love you and I had two who were in love with me.

Not long after my exchange with Rosie, Richard and Desiree

returned. If the situation were reversed, Richard would've turned Desiree down. I was angry at myself for not leaving that morning at Rosie's place. It was too late to lament over it now.

Rosie had fabricated a story when Richard returned from the tour and asked her what she did. She told him that it didn't feel right to go swimming without him, so she pretended she didn't feel well. She also told him that I was a gentleman and that I offered to stay with her, but she insisted that I go to the beach alone. I was so tired, I wanted to sleep, but Desiree wanted to have sex so bad. A gentleman has to please his lady always.

On the last night before our departure we were all gathered, having a few drinks at one of the bars at the resort. Rosie constantly argued with me that night. It was obvious to Desiree that she was upset with me. Desiree even asked her what was going on and why she was so mean to me. Rosie dismissed the question by pretended she was drunk. She apologized. The night went on without any more arguing but I knew she was just upset she didn't hear what she wanted the other day when she asked me about my feeling for Desiree.

I was so distracted. My situation was complicated. I was married; I knew that I should forget about Rosie and focus on my family. I had an attractive wife who loved me. It was so simple: all I had to do was love her back and my life would be great. My selfish heart had a different story. I wanted both Rosie and Desiree. I wanted them to continue loving me regardless of who might get hurt.

CHAPTER SEVEN

RICHARD AND ROSIE had purchased a house about ten miles away from my house. During the summer, we played tennis and racquetball at the club almost every weekend. Rosie was still giving me the cold shoulder when she saw me. I didn't care anymore. Bryan turned one. I took him to the park almost every afternoon to the swing, which he loved.

Richard had been so happy. He told me that since there was no school, he was not being neglected sexually by Rosie anymore. He also told me that Rosie was late with her period. Richard was delighted when Rosie's doctor confirmed that she was two months pregnant.

Desiree was not herself lately. She was tired, and found herself throwing up in the morning. She made an appointment to see her doctor, who confirmed that she was also two months pregnant. It was always a dream for Desiree and Rosie to be pregnant at the same time. We wanted the babies to be born the same month. Our dreams had come true.

I was happy to know that I was going to have a second child. But Desiree's first pregnancy also meant goodbye to sex for almost nine months for me. Surprisingly, with this current pregnancy, Desiree was always in the mood for sex.

These days Rosie and Desiree were inseparable. Going to the mall was their daily activity. On days when they weren't together, we always managed to bump into Rosie and Richard. He always had a smile on his face.

I hated the mall and constantly complained to him, but Richard loved being with Rosie, even if he had to endure the torture of her getting dressed and undressed at every shop they went into, even when she did not plan on buying anything. Richard just smiled. I was different. Everyone in the mall would notice my discomfort.

Desiree was in her ninth month. Her belly was so big that we felt the baby could come at any time. On Sunday, March 10, 1991, she was in terrible pain and nothing seemed to ease it. I gave her a back-rub and we did breathing exercises, but nothing worked; she was very uncomfortable. She started to bleed, and I called her doctor. He urged us to go to the hospital.

After Desiree was admitted I called Richard to tell him about the situation. There was no answer. Desiree was placed on oxygen and the baby was monitored closely. As she rested, I went to the hospital cafeteria. I found Richard there having lunch.

"How come you're here?"

"Rosie is having her baby. Why are you here?"

"Desiree was just admitted."

"Let's go check on them both when we're finished eating."

By the time we went to check on them, the nurses had been looking for Richard. Rosie was fully dilated and ready to give birth. I was kicked out of the room, so I went straight to Desiree's room where she was still sleeping.

I paced back and forth between Desiree's room and Rosie's. I was anxious to know that everything was going fine. One hour later, Richard came out.

"I am a proud papa of a nine-pound boy, Richard Junior."

"Congratulations!"

I gave him a hug and told him I was going back to check on Desiree.

Desiree was in labor for ten hours. I prayed she would be okay. When Patricia finally came into this world we were very happy. Desiree decided to do a tubal ligation; she felt that she did not want to have any more children after this one.

Richard and I couldn't believe our babies were born on the same day. Since he had the boy and I had the girl, we said we'd make sure they got married to each other when they got older.

During the fall semester, after our babies were born, our wives decided to go back to school. Desiree went back to New Paltz, the state university about four miles from our house. Rosie went back to a school in New York City. Most of the time, since I worked in Westchester County, I dropped her off at Columbia University and she took the metro north and Richard picked her up from the train station.

One Saturday morning, Richard took his son to visit his uncle. Desiree and I were home when Richard called to let us know that Rosie needed a ride home. Her car had broken down on the highway. She had called a tow truck, so I came to take her home.

This time I was the aggressor. She had on a tight miniskirt. I couldn't resist those legs next to me. I started to caress them without asking. I pulled over next to a secluded old house.

I got out of the car and reclined the passenger seat all the way back. I pulled up her miniskirt and started to kiss her panties. I gently pulled her panties to one side. I slipped my tongue on her clit. She was already so wet. It didn't take her long to start moving her hips slowly. The deeper I penetrated with my tongue, the faster she moved. She held my head tight between her thighs. She was so shocked about the moment that she remained speechless for the rest of the car ride until we reached her place.

As I was getting ready to drive away, she said, "Aren't you coming in? Richard will not be home until later. Don't you want reciprocity?"

I parked the car, went to the guest room, and took all my clothes off. Rosie made a call to make sure Richard was away. She took all her clothes off too and jumped on top of me. I busted inside of her so fast. It was as if I hadn't had sex for three years.

Most of the time when we had sex I pulled out, but this day was exceptional because I wanted her so bad. She said not to worry. She had planned to take birth control pills. She just needed to pick them up at the pharmacy.

We had sex almost every day for the next few weeks. We made all kinds of excuses to meet. She knew when Desiree was working so I would go pick up the kids late. She came to my house a couple of times. Sometimes we would meet on a deserted street and make love. We were like two teenagers who had just discovered how good it was to have sex and we wanted to do it all the time.

I never understood how Rosie managed to be Desiree's best friend. Maybe Rosie's manipulative tactics were the reason Desiree never suspected our love affair. She pretended that she could not stand me. Ever since that night, the last one at the resort during her honeymoon, she made it clear to everyone that we didn't like each other.

Rosie let Richard believe that we barely talked during our car rides. Richard used to apologize to me for her behavior. He said I was a true friend for driving her despite her dislike of me. I reached a point where I didn't feel guilty about the situation anymore. I convinced myself that it was natural to love Rosie and that it would never be more because of our marital situations.

I was the man with two hearts. I loved both women the same way and they both loved me too. I often thought about the unfairness of life. One person might go through life looking for reciprocal love and never find it. Other people might think they'd found it, while in reality it was not reciprocal—this was the case with Richard and Rosie.

Look at me, two timing with two true loves. I must have been the luckiest man on Earth to be loved by two people at the same time. I loved both of them dearly. If someone asked me to choose I would not have been able to do it. My life would be incomplete without them. Just like a day starts with the sun and blends to night and the sight of the moon, my life needed both of them to be happy. Especially on the days that I spent with both of them separately, I saw that each one had a unique way of satisfying my needs. I got jealous for both of them. I missed both of them at times, and I would do anything for them.

Three months later, Desiree told me that Rosie was three months pregnant. I called Rosie and asked her to meet me. Rosie and I had ways of communicating so people would never know that we were talking to each other. When I called her on the phone, if I said hello twice it meant to meet me half an hour later by our spot down the street from her house. If she answered hello with my name it meant that Richard was there. If she answered hello without saying my name, Richard was there and it would not be possible to meet; then she would call me later and arrange a meeting time.

Once I heard the news from Desiree that Rosie was pregnant, I was panicking silently, thinking that baby could be mine given the amount of unprotected sex Rosie and I were having. I called her to meet with me because I was concerned that the baby could be mine. She told me that she and Richard rarely had sex, but she was confident it wasn't mine. She was taking birth control pills every day as prescribed during the time we were having sex. She did recall that the last month she had missed a few days of taking the pills, but she was only having sex with Richard at the time. She claimed afterwards I didn't care about her. It made her very upset that I called her only for that. I reminded her that I was married and would not jeopardize that with anyone. I didn't want Desiree to find out about us.

Rosie said, "You meet me all the time, you fuck me, then what?"

I said: "I thought we both enjoyed being together. We're both married and best friends with each other's spouses. What else would we want from each other?"

She knew that I was telling the truth, but didn't like the answer. She started to sob and said, "I've been used by you. I stayed away from you and you pulled me back in your life only to humiliate me and degrade me."

"I'm sorry you feel that way," I said. Then I extended my hands from the passenger seat to give her a comforting hug.

She screamed loudly, "Don't you dare touch me. You're right, I should've known before I had sex with you that you would never stand by me. I let myself fall in love with the wrong man. I don't ever want to see you again."

I was trying again so hard to reason with her but it was in vain.

She said violently, "Get out of my car now. I mean it this time. No more sneaking around to see you. What for? If you care about me at all, you'll stay away from me forever and give me a chance to love Richard as he deserves to be loved. I'm going to stay away from you and never look back. You should do the same."

I'd never felt so hurt in my life. I didn't do anything to be treated like that. I knew we were both in it together, but I never expected that reaction out of her. For the rest of the year, I did what she asked me to do. I stayed away. It was the hardest thing I had to do because I missed her terribly.

On October 17, 1992, Rosie also gave birth to a girl named Abigail. I remember one day as I was driving her to school, Rosie had asked me if I were to have more children what my favorite names were for a boy and a girl. I said Charles and Abigail. I shouldn't have been surprised when she named the baby Abigail. She said she chose the name because I could no longer have children with Desiree.

I was concerned Abigail was mine and perhaps she'd argued with me to keep me away. If I weren't around it wouldn't raise suspicion just in case the baby looked like me. I was happy when I heard the baby looked exactly like Richard's mother.

For the next five years, Rosie and I hardly had a real conversation. When we saw each other it was always with our spouses or with our children. We became casual friends—a slight upgrade from being enemies. She was still mad at me about that last argument. I never stopped thinking about her.

I came to realize that she never loved me. Every time I saw her it felt like a bulldozer was crushing my heart. I was miserable, but also it allowed me to focus only on Desiree and my children.

Desiree and I took night classes together at Mount Saint Mary College, a local college, where we completed our master's degrees in nursing to become nurse practitioners. Rosie had achieved her dream of becoming a fully licensed psychologist and Richard completed his doctorate in physical therapy.

We continued to support each other. Our children were good friends. They had sleepovers all the time. Richard and I continued our routine of working out together. I changed jobs and worked in the same local hospital with Richard; we had similar schedules.

Eventually, Rosie and I agreed to put our differences aside during the tenth birthday party we had for Richard Junior and Patricia. We realized that our children got along so well that we should do better. She told me that she was very hurt during that last time we met in the car, but it was forgiven. I tried to block her out of my mind by focusing on Desiree, but I couldn't because I still loved her. When I knew it was really over between Rosie and me, I felt betrayed.

She avoided any opportunity to be alone with me. I became desperate for her love. I decided that I needed someone to talk to and I asked my doctor to give me a referral to have her treat me.

I scheduled a visit with her. Now I would finally address the issues that tormented me. I was so anxious to see her that I didn't sleep the night before. I wanted her back in my life. I missed that spontaneity that she used to bring to my life. I needed her.

I arrived early to fill out insurance-related forms. My heart was beating so loudly. I was scared. I was directed to a waiting room, and I waited anxiously for my beautiful Rosie. There was a knock at the door; it was Dr. Rosenberg. He said Rosie could not see me because of our friendship. She had asked him to see me instead.

I was furious. I got up politely and left without saying anything. I felt insulted. She could've called me herself and told me. I took this as a sign that she clearly didn't want me anymore. I swallowed my pride and stayed away for good.

On April 3, 2003, Richard's father passed away. Richard was close to his father and he was devastated by the loss. I did everything that I could to help him through it. He was happy that I was always there to cheer him up. I made sure that there was always a program on, mostly comedy shows or Knicks games—something to do to avoid being depressed.

Richard's father left him a lot of money, but he never talked about it. Six months after his father's death, Richard decided that he didn't want to work in the hospital anymore. He had enough money to open his own physical therapy clinic.

Richard proposed that we go into business together. Richard and Rosie had invited Desiree and me to dinner to discuss the deal. We concluded that we would buy a building and transform it into a clinic where patients could receive care.

Richard and Rosie served as the majority partners because they had more money invested. Richard was delighted to see us doing business together. He said we were fifty/fifty partners. We called the place The Desired Rose Healthcare and Rehabilitation Center, after the names of our spouses, Desiree and Rosie. It officially opened May 15, 2004.

While we were working at the hospital, we met several medical doctors, nurse practitioners, nurses, therapists, and other healthcare workers willing to work with us. We started the business with fifteen employees.

Rosie relocated her practice to the same building. We were very happy together. The staff was very happy about our fairness toward them and the patients were very happy with the services they were receiving. The place was a brand new facility, much needed in the area.

Richard and I had the keys to the building. Most nights, we stayed late to close and we decided who would open the next day.

The business was going very well for us. The following year, Richard hired two new physical therapists, James and Alex. He spent most of his afternoon time with his son Richard, who turned fourteen and was playing basketball for his high school. Richard never missed a game. One night, I was closing the place after I thought all the staff had gone. I saw a light on in Rosie's office. I knocked on her door and she was still there.

I asked Rosie how much time she needed before I closed. She said to lock the front door because she had something to tell me. I went and locked the door.

I went to her office and found Rosie was leaning against a table on her hands, wearing only her underwear. She had no idea how much I wanted her. I didn't say a word; I knew what to do. I went straight to her breasts and gently kissed them.

My heart was racing; it had been such a long time. Her body hadn't changed with age—or was it my dick that was thinking? I took off my pants and laid her on a big chair and made sweet, tender love to her. We must have forgotten where we were because we were screaming.

Later she confessed that she and Richard had not had sex for almost a year. She had lost interest and he had noticed. He used to try to sleep with her, but after a while he had given up.

Two weeks earlier when Richard told me that he'd lost interest in sex and had problems getting an erection, I told him about some natural foods and drinks that were aphrodisiacs. He told me that Rosie had been so frustrated with him that he no longer tried. I wanted to prescribe something for him, but he refused. I knew then it would be just a matter of time before she would come to me; I was very patient.

For the following three years, up to 2008, the health center generated more money than we expected. We doubled the number of employees and our wives rarely came to the center anymore. Desiree worked four hours in the morning, twice a week. Rosie worked only three times a week at night, by appointment only. Bryan was delighted when he was accepted at Columbia University. Patricia and Richard were in their last year of high school and Abigail had almost given Richard a heart attack when he saw a boy kissing her during her sweet sixteen birthday party.

Richard opened every morning to make sure the staff was there. Then he would leave to attend his children's games, or other business. I would often come in during the afternoon and make sure everyone left.

Then I would close the place.

On Mondays, Wednesdays, and Fridays, Rosie and I had our rendezvous. We liked to role-play. One day she was my psychologist and I was her nurse practitioner. Another day, I was her gynecologist and her receptionist at the same time. I massaged her clit with one hand while my other hand held the phone pretending to give directions to a patient.

One time, when I had my thumb and forefinger massaging her clit while another finger was in her vagina, she decided where she needed an injection with my big syringe, in her mouth or her vagina. Every now and then we used to do something different to keep it exciting.

James was one of the therapists Richard had hired almost four years earlier. He was the type that always made sure his work was completed each day before leaving. He was a very good worker who took pride in his work. One particular Friday, I thought he had left the facility when I closed as usual. I was so anxious to get to Rosie that I overlooked his station. He saw us coming out of Rosie's office; we were sweaty, fixing our clothes in the hallway. Although the door had been locked, we made a lot of noise. Our appearance made it obvious that we were doing some kind of other work. He was shocked and gave us a look of disgust. He left without saying a word to us.

Rosie and I panicked. We worried that James would start a rumor about us. We didn't sleep all night. The next day, I ran to the office before Richard to catch James in case he was there. I wanted to say something to him. I spent the whole day at the office, but James didn't show up to work.

My anxiety ran sky high; I didn't know if I could take the pressure until Monday. I told Richard that I had nothing to do on Monday so I could open the place if he had something to do. Luckily he had to visit his doctor Monday and already had planned to ask me to open.

On Monday morning I started earlier than usual. I was nervous about meeting with James. When he arrived I was the first one to greet him. He barely looked at me. He walked to his area quickly. After he settled down, I told him I wanted to have a word with him in my office.

Fifteen minutes later, he came to my office.

I said, "You know why I called you in here? It's about Friday."

"I am here to work, not to have any problems with anyone. I don't usually put my nose in anybody's business. Richard is a good guy. I hope what I thought I saw was just my imagination. I'll leave it at that. If for any reason it was not my imagination, I mean to say that if it occurs again, I will let him know." He added, "For your information, I saw the two of you before hugging tightly. I knew there was something more. Richard is your best friend and he regards you highly, so I know you will do the right thing."

He got up and walked out to his station. I wanted to tell him that he had no right to accuse me of something that he was not sure about. I told him I'd let it go.

Rosie and I had no intention of stopping. It was true love for us. I questioned the love we had for our spouses. Did it warrant the suffering of Richard? I called Rosie and told her about the conversation I had with James. Rosie was upset because I didn't defend her in front of James. I told her it was a fair warning. She and I had been playing with fire and it was only a matter of time before we got burned.

Rosie and I got smarter regarding our relationship. We were looking for a place to rent. Rosie had an old friend from college who had a condo for rent because she had accepted a position offered by the United Nations in South Africa. Rosie and I rented the place. Rosie scheduled her visits while Richard was at the health center, and would leave early for four hours every Tuesday and Thursday. Richard trusted her so much that he never once questioned her when she said something to him. She told Richard that on Tuesdays she had yoga class and swimming and on Thursdays she was volunteering, teaching a class on public speaking. I told Desiree that I was helping my friend by coaching Little League on Tuesdays. Thursdays, I signed up for an indoor soccer club. I begged Desiree to come with me when I was signing up, so she knew or perhaps had an idea where I was every Thursday. I never returned to the place after I signed up; soccer was never my thing. Tuesdays and Thursdays we met at our new place. Now that we had a new place, we didn't make love every time we met.

We cooked, played together, and slept in each other's arms most of the time. When it was time to leave, I was always heartbroken because we enjoyed each other's company so much.

CHAPTER EIGHT

ROSIE AND I were suffering in silence. We loved each other so much, but also had our obligations to fulfill with our spouses. I found myself not too interested sexually in Desiree. She noticed that I was always tired and looking for excuses not to have sex with her. She would wear that Victoria's Secret lingerie, but I barely noticed. She would do everything she could to get my attention and show how much she wanted me. She would beg me to have sex with her, but I told her that I was not in the mood. One night, while I was sleeping, she pulled my dick out, she sucked it hard, and then she sat on it. I thought it was Rosie and was about to call her name. Good thing it was dark. I caught myself right away because Rosie and I always made love with the light on.

Our situation began to grate on Desiree's confidence on a daily basis. She thought that she was no longer able to satisfy me anymore. She thought that perhaps I no longer found her attractive. She decided to take matters to her best friend, Rosie, her most trusted adviser. She called Rosie on a Thursday afternoon, while Rosie and I were cooking at our place, and left her a voicemail.

"Rosie, I have something very important to discuss with you. Make sure to call me; it is urgent and cannot wait for tomorrow."

Seriously, that phone call spoiled the rest of our afternoon. We weren't sure what it was all about. Rosie and I were retracing everything to make sure that we hadn't committed any mistakes and been caught.

Rosie called her back to see what the phone call was about. She said that she would rather wait and discuss it face to face with her. Rosie agreed to meet with her later that night.

Rosie felt that she was unlucky given the way her life was going. She always showed a different façade to people when they asked her about her relationship with Richard. She always painted him as the world's greatest husband, father, and lover. The way she used to go on and on about him used to make me feel so jealous, until I realized she used to make up stories as a cover. When out in public, her hands were always all over him, even when the children where around. She would sit on him, feed him, and kiss him to express to people how happy she was to have Richard as a husband. It was a different story when she was with me afterward:

"It was just an act to let him believe he is the only one. Phil my love, you are my number one, baby."

Rosie was so nonchalant about the whole thing that I often wondered if she really cared about Richard or me. She often told me that she was living her wildest fantasy life. I was the one always worried about getting caught, not her. She told me that she would be happy if we did so we wouldn't have to hide anymore.

When Desiree told her that they had to talk face to face, that was the first time Rosie showed me a sense of panic. She was pacing back and forth and questioning me reluctantly about what Desiree might ask her. She told me that she didn't want her friendship with Desiree to change.

She left me in the apartment and drove to my house to meet with Desiree. My daughter Patricia was home, so they decided to go to a coffeeshop in the neighborhood. Rosie told me later that it was the first time she felt so nervous because she knew she was screwing her best friend's husband and she felt that Desiree might be suspicious. But she kept silent during the ride.

"What it is, Desiree?" asked Rosie as they were sitting down after ordering smoothies.

"I think Phil doesn't love me anymore."

"That's silly, what makes you say that? He adores you," replied Rosie.

"It's never happened before that Phil goes two weeks without having sex with me—and now we're going on a month. I tried everything I can. I bought new lingerie and renovated the bedroom by transforming it into a romantic and exotic place as he once told me that he would like the bedroom to be. He barely noticed the new changes. I am going crazy. I love Phil.

"How do you do it, Rosie? You always tell me how you and Richard have sex all the time, at least two to three times a week. Please tell me the secret so Phil can find me irresistible as before."

Rosie felt relief that Desiree had no clue she was the reason why I didn't want her anymore.

"No my dear, men go through the same thing that women often go through. It is called a mid-life crisis. Once they hit forty, they want to show to the world that they are still young and have it. You told me that he just bought a brand new convertible. I don't think Phil is the cheating type. Maybe his libido has decreased? Just give him some time, perhaps a little romantic vacation, just the two of you in his new car. I know one thing: he loves you and his children very much. Just be patient."

Desiree was very happy with the advice that Rosie had given

her. She thanked her and they hugged each other. After dropping off Desiree back at her house, Rosie was thinking about their conversation. For the first time, she looked at the relationship from Desiree's side and felt that she was hurting her when she was spending time with me. For the first time her conscience had finally come into play and made her feel ashamed of what we were doing. She questioned herself as a professional therapist. She was treating patients everyday with some marital problems and other problems. She always found the right treatment for them, yet she couldn't cure her own heart of this ongoing dilemma in her life. Desiree's lamentation had touched her; she finally admitted to herself, "I am wrong for doing this to her and Richard. They deserve better." Rosie called me to let me know that we had to talk at an emergency meeting the next day.

Honestly, I couldn't sleep. I was waiting for tomorrow to come. I saw that Desiree was extra nice that night to me, and I got scared. I'd been around her long enough to know that when she was that nice, something was cooking, and she was preparing a trap for me. I pretended to go along with her game. I made love to her that night, I licked every inch of her body, and I made her scream so loud that I realized how much she had wanted me.

Desiree was so happy about the night. As soon as my daughter went to school, she noticed that I was downstairs making breakfast. She came downstairs wearing nothing but a thong. She looked very sexy. As she was coming down each step, she stopped and turned her backside so I could see her shaking her butt like a dance tease. By the time she reached the last step, I ran to her, carried her to the island, spread her legs, and was devouring her pussy with my tongue for breakfast. After she came I carried her to the family room sofa and fucked her like there was no tomorrow. We fell asleep exhausted on the sofa for two hours. I was so preoccupied with Rosie that I had neglected my wife; I felt bad.

She completed the breakfast that I barely started and asked me if we could take a week or two off and drive to Texas, just the two of us in my new car. I told her that I had to talk with Richard and the other staff members to cover our patients' caseload and I would let her know.

By then Rosie had called me and left me several messages. I finally answered her and told her that I was sleeping. We agreed to meet at our place later that afternoon. I was not worried anymore because whatever the meeting Rosie had with Desiree was about, it sure didn't involve me; otherwise there was no way that Desiree would have been so hot with me like that. Rosie and I met as promised later on. She felt a little coldness on my part as she was kissing me. "You fucked Desiree last night, didn't you?"

"Is that what this emergency meeting is all about?" I asked her.

"I am not happy about it, but it is okay," she said.

"It is okay?" I asked. "Really? What are you talking about? Are you okay?"

"I talked to Desiree last night and realized how much I was hurting her. She is too good a friend to me to hurt her like that. You were right all the time, from the first day when you were asking me about Richard. Now I know how you feel. My conscience has finally tormented me all night. I love you too much, Phil; I hope you know that's the only reason I've been with you all these years and the only reason why I have to let you go unconditionally back to Desiree."

Tears were pouring from Rosie's eyes. I hugged her and cleaned her tears with my handkerchief. I started to kiss her, and she closed her eyes, her mouth open for my tongue. The fact that I'd had such exquisite sex with Desiree the night before and that morning again meant that somehow I didn't feel Rosie. She was hoping to make love with me for the last time. I pretended that I was so hurt by her comment that my body was shut down at that moment.

I quickly changed the subject. "Desiree asked me to go on a trip, just the two of us."

"You should go, take her. Go have a good time with her. After all, she is your wife," Rosie replied.

Rosie left, frustrated and disappointed. I had already told Richard the circumstances between Desiree and me. As a true friend, he said everything would be under control and I should go and have a good time. I dropped my daughter off at his house. For the following two weeks, Desiree and I renewed the passion and love in our marriage from New York to Houston, Texas, to our last stop at Desiree's mother's house; she had relocated from California. We made love from the rest areas to the hotels that we stayed in. We had a chance to visit all the places we wanted to visit before but never were able to. We were holding hands, kissing each other all the time like two young lovers who had just discovered love. I never once thought about Rosie while I was away with Desiree, until we reached the sign: "Welcome to New York." Desiree was sleeping and I was wondering how the relationship with Rosie was going to be now.

We arrived very late. My daughter Patricia told me that she didn't want to come back home because she had such a good time with Rosie and Abigail. Desiree went to talk privately with Rosie. I didn't care. Richard was very happy for me and said that hopefully he and Rosie could do the same in the near future. I gave them all the souvenirs that we had brought for them.

For the following two months after the trip, things were great between Desiree and me. We made more time to go out to the movies, restaurants, and dancing. I told her that the indoor season was over and the Little League team was on vacation. I didn't hear from Rosie and was not interested to find out.

One afternoon, as I was about to pump gas in the car, my cellphone rang. It was Rosie.

"How are you doing stranger? You are having such a great time with your wife that you have forgotten about me. Remember she is my best friend and she told me everything."

"How are you, Rosie?"

"Not even a phone call, Phil? I feel like such a fool."

"No," I said, "you shouldn't feel like that. Remember we talked about this and you suggested that it was the right thing to do."

"I know, but I never thought that you would do a 360 degrees on me like that, Phil.

We have to meet and discuss the apartment."

Although I knew it was a bad idea, I agreed to it. As soon as I saw her, everything went back to normal. We made love all afternoon; I had to call and cancel my dentist appointment. We left without mentioning a word about the apartment. I told Desiree that the indoor soccer season had resumed and Little League too. She was very disappointed, but we agreed to spend time together on the weekends.

For almost a year, my Tuesday/Thursday routine with Rosie was reincarnated. Desiree was neglected again. As a matter of fact, I'd been telling her that most weekends now, the team traveled to play at different locations. That was extra time I was spending with Rosie. She told Richard that she had a new class she was teaching for her friend on Saturdays because she was on maternity leave. Sexually, life was great for me.

Desiree had met with one of her old friends from the hospital who became her patient. During a conversation, she told Desiree that her son was involved in Little League; the coach was her brother. She said she was always in the park with them. She knew all the staff, and said there was no way that I was part of it when Desiree mentioned my name and described me to her. She also mentioned that the YMCA that used to have the indoor soccer team had closed the previous year. Desiree had driven to the place later that day and found out that her friend was telling the truth.

Desiree was not the type to confront you right away when she noticed something was wrong. She would make sure to gather all her facts, so when she came to you, you would have no excuse. Desiree's suspicion had increased. She began to call the center, investigating what time I came and left. She stopped there several times herself and I was nowhere to be found. She went to the park where I told her that the Little League team played and it was empty. I was with Rosie in our apartment. She paid a private investigator, who followed me. Within a week he revealed to Desiree that I definitely was having an affair. He gave Desiree pictures of me and Rosie kissing; luckily my face was visible, but she couldn't see Rosie's face clearly. Desiree went to her best friend Rosie with all the facts and told her that she was going to file for divorce. She told Rosie that from the first day, she had told me that she would tolerate everything from me except cheating. Rosie was shocked and told her to think about it at least for a week before she decided to do that.

Rosie warned me the same night. I told her that we had to stop seeing each other because I had to save my marriage. I told Rosie that I loved Desiree the same as I loved her; the only difference was that Desiree and I had two kids together. I told Rosie that if she wanted to leave me I would be crushed with hurt but I would never leave Desiree and my children for her. Rosie was disappointed by my feelings. Rosie once again felt betrayed by me. She developed an instant hate for me and vowed never to see me again. This time I was ready. I was finally ready to confess to Desiree, to get a marriage counselor, and to move out of the area.

Desiree called Rosie and told her that she was not going to wait for a week and that our marriage was over. She told Bryan and Patricia that I betrayed our marriage by having an affair. Desiree had contacted a lawyer and began the process of our divorce. My children were upset with my behavior, and confronted me, asking me to tell them who and why. I couldn't say a word to them. They didn't want to have anything to do with me. Bryan told me he admired my love for his mother and he would never believe what he heard about me. Patricia was more forgiving about the situation but she was disappointed by my actions. She told me that she would talk to her mother, since I'd been such a great father. It would be a long shot because Desiree's mind was made up.

When I got to the house that night, I felt that my life, my dreams, everything was being taken from me. I was blinded by the love I had for Rosie. I should have ended it before the whole thing blew up in my face like this. Desiree told me to move out. She said that our marriage was over. I tried to talk to her. I begged her to give me a chance, but it was too late.

CHAPTER NINE

I CHECKED IN at the hotel down the street for a month while I waited to see if Desiree would reconsider. I talked to everyone who knew us. I asked them to talk to her and make her change her mind, but it was in vain.

Eventually, I rented a two-bedroom apartment. Richard harassed Desiree with several phone calls a day to take me back. She said, "never." Richard met with her so he could influence her into giving me a second chance. She told Richard that she was heartbroken, and she could never trust me again. She had made it clear to me before and throughout our marriage that cheating was one mistake that she would never forgive me for.

The funny thing was that Richard remained a loyal friend to me. Here I was cheating with his wife and he constantly spoke with Desiree on my behalf without me knowing. I didn't ask him to intervene on my behalf because I knew I was wrong. He told me he would do anything to see my marriage with Desiree work out. Here I was destroying his marriage at the same time. I was happy Desiree had chosen not to know whom I was cheating with; otherwise she and Richard would have sung a different tune.

At the same time Desiree was being neglected, things were not so great in Richard's household. Rosie was not even sleeping in the same bed with Richard anymore. They knew their marriage was just a façade. The children often witnessed the neglect of their father but hid it well so no one outside the family had a clue that things were not working between their parents. Richard Junior would ask his dad why he put up with her at times. Rosie became so careless with her family. She would go out, stay out late, and no one knew her whereabouts. I could always tell the times when everything was going well in Richard's house, and he was happy. Those were the moments mostly when Rosie and I were not seeing each other. He would come to the center with a more casual look, smiling, laughing, and had his famous quote, "Love is in the air," when people would ask him what was going on. He always told people how grateful he was to have Rosie as his wife and he attributed all their success to working hard together. Rosie had not been going out in public with Richard for a while. On rare occasions they would celebrate their children's birthdays together in a public space. Rosie had been feeling guilty knowing that she was a big part of the mess going on with my life.

Rosie had mentioned to me on several occasions that the love she felt for Richard was not real. She had reached a point in her life where she got in touch with her conscience and realized that Richard could still find someone to truly love him. I hoped she was not thinking that because Desiree and I were divorcing I would be with her if she left Richard. I would never let that happen. I would consider moving to a different state rather be with her under such circumstances. I was imagining the cruel things friends, family, our children, Richard, Desiree, and people in general would have said to us.

Rosie had invited Richard to a new French restaurant down the street from their house. He told me to close the clinic that afternoon. He planned to have dinner with his wife at Le Chateau. He told me that it had been a while since the two of them did something romantic and that he was very excited. I was very happy for him. I was hoping that Rosie really had a change of heart, realizing what a great guy Richard was and would start to treat him that way.

I was so focused on having one more chance with Desiree that I forgot about Rosie. In fact, I had been thinking about all the times I spent with Rosie. They were truly nothing but good times, but she had manipulated the situation from day one. If Rosie had never been in my life that way, Desiree and I still would have been together. I blamed myself for not running away the very first time when I had the opportunity. Even after the second time when we realized it was a mistake, I should have stayed firm and never gone back to her. I guess sex was too good between me and Rosie to avoid that path.

For the first time in my life I had trouble sleeping. I wanted to see Desiree, to touch her, to make love to her one more time. I wanted to tell her that I was a fool for committing such stupid acts. All I needed with her was one more chance to explain my pain to her, to tell her that I loved her and willing to do anything, whatever the cost, to see us reunited again.

I was recently on top of Mount Everest, invincible with two burning love fires, one on each side. Both of the women hated me now and I never thought that it would come down to me being so desperate. I was trying hopelessly to resuscitate my love that was on life support. I felt that I was about to take my last breath of love with Desiree.

The next day, I didn't go to work as early as usual. I didn't hear from Richard; he always called me to brag after having a good time out with Rosie. Perhaps because of my divorce with Desiree he didn't think it would be appropriate to brag as before.

I walked to the clinic and found Richard in his office. I went to him and shook his hand. I noticed a sad and an unusual look on his face, like he was recently crying. I asked him what had happened. He told me that Rosie told him their marriage was a mistake. She said that she was never truly happy because she thought she had married the wrong man.

She went on to tell him that she always loved him but it was only forty percent over the years and that her love decreased year after year. She told him that he was still young and he could find someone else to love him.

Richard was a great guy and he deserved one hundred percent of love. She didn't want him to send any friends or any family members to mend things. Her mind was made up and she was no longer in love with him or even loved him anymore.

I was ready to go to Rosie, but Richard begged me not to talk to her. Richard had asked me to open and close the clinic for the rest of the week while he went to his uncle's house. When he returned later that week he stayed with me until he found an apartment.

He already had a copy of my apartment key, so instead of returning it to me, he gave me a copy of his apartment key, which was a half an hour away from mine. We wanted to be able to check on each other. We were both depressed and worried, but not stupid.

Rosie and Desiree no longer went to the clinic. The atmosphere at work was not the same. It was just a place I went to in order to help me forget about the negativity in my life. I found myself thinking about what I should've done or could've accomplished. Rumors at work circulated about why our marriages had failed.

I lost all hope when Desiree officially served me with divorce papers. I told Richard that I was not going to fight with her regarding anything. She could have whatever she wanted. Richard said he would not let Rosie off the hook that easily. He started to think Rosie might have someone new. I got jealous a little. I did not think he was referring to me. I encouraged him to check. He said he was going back to check old bills and phone numbers from last year. I discouraged him from doing that. Richard never once asked about my affair until when we went to a bar one night.

I told him it was someone who I met a long time ago, but that it was not as significant as Desiree had made it seem. Richard thought Rosie left him because he had not been able to perform sexually. He told me that he made an appointment to see a doctor regarding new treatments to give him a new sexual life again. He wanted to go back to Rosie and fix his marriage. I was happy that he was so determined to make his marriage work. I wouldn't dare tell him that when the heart dies nothing else matters.

Not long after, I asked Richard about his doctor's appointment. He told me that it went well. His doctor had sent blood work to determine if he qualified for new medications. The doctor said his prostate might be a factor. Richard and I continued to give each other support but we knew people around us had noticed something was missing between us.

Richard and I played tennis once in a while, and we went to a bar weekly. We were two

men hit by midlife crisis in search of a little happiness. We went to bar sometimes, thinking we still had it with women. Truthfully our hearts were broken because the love we had for our spouses was irreplaceable. I knew it was time to move on from Desiree after the divorce was final. But not Richard. He was determined to have Rosie back.

CHAPTER TEN

OUR CHILDREN WERE no longer small. Patricia and Bryan were attending Columbia and Ohio State Universities. Patricia was a sophomore pre-med and Bryan wanted to continue after his bachelor's degree to law school. Richard Junior was attending Long Island University to be a physical therapist just like his dad. Their youngest child, Abigail, was a freshman at Georgetown University.

Rosie was reluctant about it but she felt it was the right thing to do after twenty years of marriage, a marriage based on lies, and it was time to finally set Richard free. He was going to the house every time he had a chance in the hope of seeing Desiree, but she was never there. She and I didn't talk anymore and I was happy. I had a chance to spend more time with Richard. Perhaps one day after he met someone else, he might forgive me for what happened between Rosie and me if he ever found out. Desiree hated me with a passion. Patricia and Bryan rarely returned my calls; they were still upset about the way I treated their mother.

THE MAN WITH TWO HEARTS

On September 10, 2010, I panicked when I didn't see Richard at work. It was obvious that something was wrong. It was very unusual of him not to be present. I was thinking that he had been distant for the past two weeks. He barely talked to me. He didn't want to hang out anymore either. I became suspicious that someone like James had said something to him about Rosie and me, because rumor was all over the center.

It was the first time I didn't hear from Richard, even for very simple instructions about the clinic. He was supposed to open that morning, but he didn't show up. I had something to do for my mother, so the clinic had opened later than usual.

Now, here I was standing in Richard's apartment. He had left a note for me, as I was the only one with his key. It read:

"Thank you for your so-called friendship. I trusted you with my life. I trusted you with my family. You are nothing but a weak man and a thief. By the time you find this letter I will be at the bleacher. I will go there to be in peace with my life because at this point it is worth nothing. You have taken it all. I hope you're happy. I hope you live long so I can be a constant reminder of how you destroyed my life. My soul will be eternally tormented by your actions."

The bleacher was the place in the park where we used to take our children to play when they were young. Richard and I named the bench in the park "the bleacher" because we used to have intense discussions regarding sports while watching over the children. I drove as fast as I could. I saw the tree that Richard had once mentioned would be very accessible if someone wanted to hang himself. There was yellow tape surrounding the tree. I stood speechless. I was shaking like a leaf. I was nervous. I hoped it was not what I thought. I saw an older man sitting in the park and I asked him, "Do you know why they have this yellow tape all around that area?"

He said, "A man named Richard hanged himself earlier this afternoon; it was all over the news. Didn't you hear about it?"

I went to the car and cried. I felt sick to my stomach. I wanted to die, too. I gathered myself after half an hour and went to see Rosie to find out what had happened. I was hoping maybe it was a different Richard. His house was located in a cul-de-sac. The area was always quiet, but that day the street was full with parked cars leading to his driveway. As I approached closer I could hear people crying. I instantly confirmed that the man in the park was right.

I rang the bell. Richard Junior came out.

He yelled, "Don't you dare set foot in this house. Get out! Get out!"

He closed the door in my face. I rang again and the second time Rosie came out. She shut the door behind her, tears pouring from her face. She asked me to take her somewhere private so we could talk.

I drove her to my apartment that was not too far from her house.

"Rosie, we killed Richard," I cried.

We cried for a good ten minutes. I went to the fridge and I gave Rosie a glass of water to calm her down so we could talk.

"What happened, Rosie? Why did Richard commit suicide?" I asked her.

"Richard went to a doctor who performed several blood tests for him last month. The doctor told him there was no way he could have fathered a child. Richard went to see three other doctors who told him the same thing. He did paternity tests before the kids went to college, which revealed that the doctors were telling the truth. He came to me two days ago and told me about the findings and demanded that I tell him the truth. I told him that you are the only man that I ever had sex with besides him. I told him you were the one who took my virginity. If the children were not his, then they were yours. He didn't say anything to me during the whole conversation. For the first time, I saw anger and fear in Richard's face. He furiously got up and threw a cup of coffee across the room and left without saying a word to me. That was the last time I heard from him. I was worried the way he left the house and drove away. I could hear the tires of his car screeching down the street. I didn't hear from him, so I thought that he was still mad at me. He had a right to be upset, but I never believed he would kill himself. He also wrote a letter to the children and told them that you were their father, not him. They didn't talk to me and have been avoiding me under all circumstances. I've tried to talk to them, but they looked at me with such disgust, I felt like killing myself too."

I was in shock. Rosie would not stop crying. She needed someone to talk to and asked me to drop her at her friend's house. I reassured her that she was not responsible for Richard's death, but she felt as guilty as I did.

I went to the clinic. I called all the employees and told them that the center would be closed until further notice. I also went and placed notes in front of the center doors that read, "Due to circumstances beyond our control, the center will be closed until further notice."

I went back to my apartment; I needed someone familiar with the situation to talk to. I called Desiree to tell her about Richard's death. She already knew. She was upset that Richard would let two scumbags like Rosie and me let him stop living. She said the two of us belonged together. She hoped we would burn in hell and said that I should never call her again.

I called Bryan and Patricia; Bryan told me that he didn't have a father. He said he'd rather live knowing that I was not part of his life instead of carrying the shame associated with my name. I called my mother. She said she was disappointed in my behavior. My sister would not return my phone calls; she was very upset. I had no one.

Richard was my best friend and I was the one that got blamed for his death when people found out I had an affair with Rosie. I had so many opportunities to stop cheating with Rosie, but I never did. It hit my mind that I had four children while I was thinking about the whole thing. I always had a feeling that Abigail was mine because she and Patricia had the same exact attitude, and they looked the same and got along very well.

I began to hate Rosie. If she had not come into my life, my friend still would've been alive. I hated myself for falling into her trap, for not being man enough to refuse her advances. On the contrary, I enjoyed myself. I felt invincible to be loved by two women at the same time. I was the man with two hearts and now I was the man with no heart.

I called Rosie to ask her about funeral arrangements for Richard. She said I should be prepared for negative reactions from people. There was so much I wanted to say about Richard. The children and Richard's family had left me out of the funeral arrangements, although they knew that I was the only best friend he had. I was once the most admired figured for them and I became their worst enemy after Richard died. I was debating whether or not to participate.

I decided that I should go. If I didn't show up, people would have more to say about me. The funeral was held at a church in Syracuse a week later. The church was packed with friends, family, coworkers, employees, and their families. Funerals are always sad. But Richard's funeral had everyone crying inconsolably. The combination of him being such a nice person and a wellrespected figure of his community made people feel sorry for the way that his life had ended. The saddest moment was when Richard Junior was reading his curriculum vitae; at the end, he said that his father Richard was the greatest human being he and his sister had ever known and their lives were robbed from them. Everyone was hysterically crying, including me. I turned my head to the left, and there was Desiree regarding me with a look of disbelief that dried my tears right away. I would have loved to go sit next to her, pull her closer to me, and let her cry on my shoulder, but it was too late for that; we were divorced. Abigail spoke last. She said that she didn't know what to do; she'd lost her best friend. She said their dad never once yelled at them even when they were wrong. Even his punishments were fair. She concluded with this sentence: "Heaven needed a saint, and my father responded."

Most of the people at the funeral were not aware of the reason he had hanged himself and were asking for answers. Richard's family and close friends who knew about the situation were very distant with me. Some even avoided me as I was walking toward them. I was shocked when Desiree asked to ride with me in my car to the cemetery. I knew it wasn't a good idea, but I was delighted to see her. Her purpose to ride with me was to curse me out for the last time. She went on for the entire ten-mile ride to the cemetery about the ultimate betrayal between Rosie and me. I attempted to answer her once, but she smacked me so hard that I almost got into an accident. On the way back after the burial, I saw her riding back alone in Rosie's car and I said to myself: "Rosie is in trouble."

The month after Richard's death, my life was not the same. The clinic was my only place of comfort, although it was not the same without Richard. The loyal employees who started the clinic resigned one after another.

James was the first one to resign. He told me during his last day that he knew that Richard's death must be on my conscience.

I was remorseful. I couldn't sleep. I didn't feel like living anymore. I went to see several priests and psychiatrists, but nothing worked. Even my mother made excuses not to see me or talk to me. I felt so lonely. My heart felt empty.

It was hard to find other professionals to replace the people who had resigned. Being in a small community, everyone, including patients, knew that the other owner committed suicide. My loyal patients lost confidence in me and one by one left for the new place that had recently opened. The center was falling apart rapidly, so I had no choice but to close it down six months after Richard's death. Richard made a will before he died and left all his shares of the center to his children. I sent Desiree and Rosie their shares since they were also co-owners.

I spent every day in my apartment. I used to go grocery shopping at night so I didn't have to meet anyone in the street asking me questions. I was depressed. I spent most of the day watching television, eating, or reading. My favorite show was *1000 Ways to Die*. I became so amazed and fascinated with certain techniques employed by people resulting in death. I thought about trying some of them, but I didn't have it in me. I wanted to purchase a gun, but I quickly abandoned that idea because it was too complicated.

I was begging for the daylight to arrive because at night as soon as I closed my eyes, nightmares after nightmares came. I woke up several times soaked with sweat and tears. I always found myself playing tennis or other games with Richard. I reached the point that I was scared to go to sleep. Sometimes I felt him walking in the apartment.

Almost a year to the day that Richard died, I sent a check to Rosie with all the money that I had. I also sent a letter with a detailed explanation about how to share my money between my mother, my sister, herself, and the children. I had a will and I left it with my lawyer detailing the money from the center set aside for Bryan and Patricia. I also sent a separate note to Rosie telling her goodbye. I told her that I was going to reunite with Richard in few days by the bleacher. I could no longer live with the shame surrounding Richard's death. I would follow in his footsteps.

I went to visit the tree that Richard and I had once discussed, the same tree that he used to kill himself by the bleacher. I saw that people had planted crosses and placed multiple flowers around it. I wanted to have an idea how he did it and what I would need to make it as successful as he did.

I felt the only way I could prove my sincere apology for Richard's tragedy was to do the same thing he did. I used to be one of the most outgoing and charismatic among our friends. Now, everyone hated me. Everyone from my barber to my banker had something to say to me when I saw them. The smiles, the friendly talks, the handshakes, were gone.

I saw people I knew crossing the street in the opposite direction to avoid meeting me face to face. My family hated me. He had mentioned in the note that he wanted me to live long so I could be tormented. I had already reached the maximum length of my sentence and it was not even a year yet. I saw no reason for me to continue living.

Richard had killed himself because people he knew had been cruel. He couldn't live with the shame. He had raised two children that were not his own. His best friend was cheating with his wife, a wife who never loved him. Instead of living with humiliation and the betrayal of the two people he loved the most, he found motivation to kill himself.

CHAPTER ELEVEN

THE PHONE FINALLY RANG in my apartment for the first time eleven months after Richard's death. It was Desiree.

"What do you want?" I said.

"Phil, after these few months of silence, I called you to tell you that I forgive you for all the things you and Rosie did to me. I also wanted to tell you that I met a wonderful guy and we just got married at city hall."

I hung up the phone.

❤ ❤

On September 10, 2011, exactly the one-year anniversary of Richard's death, I got up early and went to the park. Although I'm not much of a drinker, I bought a bottle of vodka and a rope and took them with me to the park.

I sat on a bench facing the tree. I contemplated how I would proceed. I started to drink the vodka slowly until half of the bottle was gone. I started to think about all the good times Richard and I used to have there. I also felt that I was ready to die. I stood up and went to the tree with a little chair that I could easily kick when I was ready. Suddenly I heard a voice that screamed, "Phil, Phil! Stop, please stop!"

It was Rosie running out of her car.

"What are you doing here?" I said.

"I know what you're about to do. I am as guilty as you are. Killing yourself is not the solution. It won't bring Richard back. I need you and I love you. You're the only person left in my life who understands what I am going through. Everyone abandoned me, including my children. People are still calling me a slut for what happened to Richard. Our four children are grown now; they don't need us anymore, but we need each other."

I looked at her intently. I couldn't believe she was really there. After all this time she needed me after all. I couldn't help it: I busted out crying, screaming like a child in a temper tantrum.

She continued, "The children are too ashamed to see us as their parents. We have enough money to live anywhere in the world. Let's go, honey. Let's go explore the world together."

We sat on the bench, where we both cried for a good half an hour. Rosie took the cord out of my hands, went to her car, put it in the trunk, and returned, sitting next to me silently.

"How did you know where I would be?" I asked her.

"Remember you sent me a letter? I drove to your house. You weren't there, and I was hoping to get here before it was too late. I lost Richard, but I don't know what I would become if I lost you too."

Rosie had convinced me not to commit suicide. What was I thinking?

She came over to my apartment; we slept for two hours. We got up, made lunch, and went to a movie out in New Jersey, where we wouldn't run into anyone we knew. That night we slept in each other's arms. It was as if we hadn't slept in decades. The next month, we decided to go away for a much-needed break. We went for a week to a resort in Mexico.

Rosie had not let me out of her sight for even a brief minute. She helped me with her technique as a psychologist to chase away those suicidal thoughts and cured me forever.

My mother was the only person who was receptive to my calls and visits. At first, she was very uncomfortable seeing me with Rosie. After a while, though she never accepted our relationship, she tolerated it because of her love for me. She kept me posted on Bryan and Patricia. They never talked to me. My mother told all four of them to have a meeting with us; after all Rosie and I are their parents. They all declined.

Rosie and I were volunteering in different places: homeless shelters, battered women's shelters, and the Red Cross. When we heard about the earthquake in Haiti on January 12, 2012, we went back to the small warehouse where we used to keep supplies for the center and sent them for help. Rosie and I decided to travel there and participate. We went with the Red Cross mission. Rosie and I were so much in love; it would have been a crime if we never had a chance to express that love. We were so happy together when we helped the people in need. They were so grateful and appreciative of us. We stayed for a month.

Rosie and I were two changed people with a quest to turn our world around. After the experience we had helping the people in Haiti, we decided to return there, only now to live permanently. We found a big piece of land in a town called Saint-Marc. The ocean was about ten miles away from us. We built a beautiful house there. We also purchased an old house in the city and transformed it into a clinic where we provided free care twice a week to the population. Rosie opened a little school and taught English to the children. We also served them food every Sunday morning. We had found a new family. The people in the town loved us. Rosie and I knew that nothing would ever replace Richard, but the kindness of our hearts and the love that we had for each other made us embrace each day as a gift.

Life is strange. Sometimes no one knows why things happen. Richard had sent me on a date with Rosie and she happened to be the love of my life. No matter what we do or how many people we meet in our lifetime, there will always be one heart.

From the start Rosie and I knew we should've been together. We took our love for granted and in the process an innocent victim paid the price. After a year of living in Haiti, I proposed to Rosie and she gladly accepted.

We sent wedding invitations to all our friends and family, including our children, six months prior to the wedding. No one ever returned our invitations. We had a small ceremony by the beach and a big party after because we had invited the whole town. Although no immediate family members came, the members of our new extended family in Haiti made it the most unforgettable memory for us. At this point in our lives, all we found is peace and harmony. Now Rosie and I have each other and that's all that matters.

THE END

Made in the USA
Charleston, SC
13 August 2016